NOT MYSELF WITHOUT YOU

D1520670

Bilingual Press/Editorial Bilingüe

Publisher

Gary Francisco Keller

Executive Editor

Karen S. Van Hooft

Associate Editors

Adriana M. Brady
Brian Ellis Cassity
Amy K. Phillips
Linda K. St. George

Address

Bilingual Press
Hispanic Research Center
Arizona State University
PO Box 875303
Tempe, Arizona 85287-5303
(480) 965-3867

NOT MYSELF WITHOUT YOU

Lourdes Vázquez

ENGLISH TRANSLATION BY **BETHANY M. KORP-EDWARDS**

Bilingual Press/Editorial Bilingüe

TEMPE, ARIZONA

Library of Congress Cataloging-in-Publication Data

Vázquez, Lourdes.
    Not myself without you / Lourdes Vázquez ; English translation by Bethany M. Korp-Edwards.
        p. cm.
    ISBN 978-1-931010-68-9 (pbk. : alk. paper)
    1. Puerto Rican families—Fiction. I. Korp, Bethany M. II. Title.
    PQ7440.V284N68 2011
    863'.64—dc22
                                                                        2010048111

PRINTED IN THE UNITED STATES OF AMERICA

Front cover art: You Feel Small Wait Until You Grow Up *(1999) by Sonya Fe*
Cover and interior design by John Wincek, Aerocraft Charter Art Service
Photos from the collection of Lourdes Vázquez

To my mother and
to the spirits who wander through Santurce.

En la palma de la mano
te quisiera retratar
Para cuando estés ausente
abrir la mano y mirar.

Acknowledgments

This novel began as an elegy in honor of two great-aunts. After their death I wrote a poem and interviewed all the members of my family. I got curious and spent many days in the library reading newspapers, government documents, and historical accounts of the period. For the witchcraft and Spiritism sections—besides my family experience—I depended on sources such as Allan Kardec's *El evangelio según el espiritismo* and *El libro de los médiums*; *Tradiciones en la brujería puertorriqueña* by Teodoro Vidal; the grimoire *El gran libro de San Cipriano*; and the infamous *Malleus Maleficarum*. The recipes are public domain; go ahead and try them. They seem to work.

Elegy

Con este corazón . . .

—LOS VAN-VAN

Who died? My mother, on the other side of the ocean, gives me the details. The great-aunts have died. One died one day, and the next day, the other died. As if one were dragging the other behind her. One flew through space and touched the other on the shoulder. That was enough for the second to understand that it was time to leave, and they left. They abandoned their photos, their souvenirs, their memories, their caring, their laughter; and in their will indicated that their ashes should be scattered in Central Park.

The aunts contracted marriage with men from Jamaica and Trinidad, and were the owners of an imperial forest of cannabis plants, which grew as tall as human beings. They lived with the conviction that the tea made from the leaves of that plant cured any ill. On holidays, they added pieces of the magic plant to bizcochos and appetizers. People felt happy. Children's laughter was transformed into birds' feathers that caressed my skin. Loving food and good music, their flesh grew until they were twin replicas of some singing Buddha.

1

One day they decided to move to New York and opened a Laundromat in the middle of Manhattan. They adored islands, and so they decided to live on this island full of rotten plagues. In their Laundromat, they cleaned up immigrants' calamities and bitterness.

"I'm not myself without you," one whispered in the other's ear. "I'm not myself; I'm someone else, someone imperfect and incomplete. I don't want to be condemned to the limbo that awaits me. Without you, I am fated to travel this highway with no exit in the midst of other souls' senile dementia. I invoke you by this heart of yours, a heart pierced with moldy ironwork; I insist: we must leave." And they left.

One unremarkable autumn afternoon I went to the park. I went in search of the ashes that were scattered across the grass, the mud, the branches, the statues, the squirrels, the fish, and the seals. Each has a cannabis flower sprouting out of its skin. Grass with a cannabis flower is understandable; what's difficult to understand is the great number of statues, fish, and seals covered with flowers.

L isten to what I tell you.] The family house was built by Abuelo Juan. It has a balcony and a garden full of marble roses, a pitched roof that in hurricane season is secured with a ship's rope, and a mahogany tree that the ocean breeze whispers through at all hours. The house was decorated by Abuela María, with help from the great-aunts. They picked out the floor tiles, with purple flowers and black leaves, which some Majorcans were selling off cheaply by the hundreds.

Everyone in the neighborhood knows that house because in the parlor Abuelo Juan founded a spiritist temple in order to relieve the souls' grievances, which are many. All the curiosity seekers who got lost in the neighborhood, and anyone who was looking for work, laid off, or unemployed (which is the same thing and doesn't matter), ends up in that parlor. The great number of witnesses to enlightened spirits there has given rise to a parade of unfortunates in search of cures for illnesses, spells to hold onto a husband, and formulas to eliminate personal misfortunes. Once the unfortunates are comforted by the spirits, they leave in a state of grace, repeating proclamations of faith and with instructions to cleanse their auras and clarify the spiritual energy of their surroundings.

Sessions are held on Tuesday nights because that is when the evil energy of the planet is most intense. They are never held during the day unless there is some kind of emergency, because during the day the island is very hot and spirits are affected by the heat, degenerating into incongruencies. Incongruent spirits are difficult to discipline, and go throughout the neighborhood frightening the elderly, children, and animals. They seize the money hidden in cookie tins; kidnap small children to play with them like ping-pong balls; kiss animals on the mouth, leaving green running sores like headless toadstools; swing from the mango trees; and produce yellow shit that they crap on houses and the cupolas of churches. All this disorder is not intentional, but rather the direct consequence of the intense steaminess that ravages the island. These phenomena have given rise to the legend that the neighborhood is bewitched.

"Fiddlesticks. It's simply that the rules of the infinite are different from the rules of the material world," was Abuelo Juan's pronouncement.

Abuelo received his first spiritist lesson on the banks of the Caño, an arm of the mangrove swamp that opens onto the sea, where all of the area's human waste ends up. At the foot of that accumulation of dirty, thick, foul-smelling water, a group of geese, pelicans, and crows (all accustomed to garbage) circle above an inferno of huts made of scraps of board, tin, and yagua branches. There are no electrical wires, no potable water, and the residents of the swamp cook funche with rice and beans over wood fires. Since there are no sewers, either, everyone shits in outhouses, and the ones who don't have outhouses go into the swamp to shit enormous feces that float away like the trunks of dwarf trees. In one section of that tunnel of water, shit, and mangrove roots, some old women have a lettuce crop. Since entre

col y col crece una lechuga, this patch is fed by a fertilizer made
of poppies, mangrove roots, magnetic powders, and bat's blood.
Make a paste and roll it into small grains. The grains should be
seared on a small stove that burns vegetable coal and laurel. To
light the fire, use a match and candle that have never been used
before. Once the fertilizer is ready, sprinkle it on the roots of the
lettuce without letting it touch the leaves, while singing to the
master and lord of the harvest: Hoja verde, hoja verde, trasmite
la verdad sin que te cueste. [Did you hear that, mi Candela?]

[Esta es la historia de un gato que tenía los pies . . .] There on
the shores of the channel, a few Haitian fishermen lived in hovels
raised up on stilts, with tin-framed windows all the way around,
looking out over the water. In the middle of the infernal stench
of the channel, in a large shack built of mature yagua branches,
they would meet every night to practice voodoo, santería, and
spiritism. Fabián was the most respected medium, and everyone would go to him to resolve any kind of problem. Abuelo
Juan would always go looking for Fabián, because matters of
witchcraft and black magic did not interest him. His passion was
the mesa blanca. Everything mi abuelo Juan knows, he owes to
Fabián, even the secret of the Rose of Jericho, [de trapo] a water-
dweller that looks like a moist spider web and that gives off a
clear secretion when it is merely touched. This secretion perme-
ates the spiritist aura, causing a fierce burning sensation. It is
especially effective against evil.

Abuela María has planted several Roses of Jericho in water
and distributed them throughout the house. You pour cool water
on the Rose of Jericho every morning to keep it alive and alert to
tribulations. The problem is that, according to the surgeon general, the water attracts the *Aedes aegypti* mosquito, so mi abuela
María had the idea of covering the vases with little scraps of silk.
The worms that make the silk have spiritual properties that have
been studied by Oriental mediums, so the clairvoyant reflections
are not affected.

Fabián also lectured Abuelo on identifying knocks on the
table and the medium's jerking, sharpening his senses of smell and
sight so that he could make out the smell of sulfur, distinguish the
secrets of lettuce leaves soaked in water, as well as finding in the
midst of the galaxy those spirits with powers sufficient to annihilate
everyday problems. Fabián left for the other life when he choked
on some pasteles made from pork rashers. Before his death, he said
not to invoke him after his death because he wouldn't come, and
that's how it has been. Fabián is never invoked in spiritist sessions
because it is known that he will not come. The ones who *can* be
invoked are Eusapia Palladino and Rosendo Matienzo Cintrón,
who henceforth will be called RMC.

Eusapia Palladino usually appears at the start of a spiritist
session or when an obsessed soul makes its entrance. She is also
the herald spirit, the one who brings good and bad news. Eusapia
Palladino has been written about by the authorities on the sub-
ject in Spain, France, England, and Italy, which are the countries
that head this movement. She is more than 4,000 years old and
has existed since the time of the first settlers in remote areas of
China. As a member of the White Brotherhood of Tibet, she made
it known that noises in the walls and furniture, dancing tables,
and a million more manifestations that today are known by the
name "spiritism" are carried out according to the instructions of
the members of that brotherhood. Because of her ethereal condition and her age, she has traveled the whole planet, meeting with
witch doctors in the Amazon and gypsies in the former Slovakia.
She possesses the wisdom of Chinese medicine, and is one of the
few spirits to know the secret of the Flower of Jericho.

For each child who was to be born in that house, Eusapia
Palladino used her spiritist powers to divine his or her personal-
ity, sex, and the problems he or she would face in life on Earth.
In this way my grandparents were forewarned of the avalanche of
children who would arrive. When Felipe was born, Eusapia Palladino divined that he had la música por dentro and they bathed him

in plants to soften his cunning; for Carmen she made a hand out of jet to repel evil intentions; she baptized Cecilia with the water from the well of the Virgin of Lourdes that is found along Highway 1 to Ponce; she hung the golden manger talisman around Claudia Luz's neck and gave instructions that for nine days her romper should be put on backwards; she wrapped Minerva in a white cloth fastened to a tortoiseshell cross soaked in rue so that her character would not be confused; for Fernando she recited the incantation of the Virgin of the River: Higo, higo, higo, la virgen del río aquí va contigo.

RMC is the spirit who personifies the politician, intellectual, liberal, Mason, spiritist, senator, exemplary husband, writer, poet, essayist, doctor, lawyer, philanthropist, lover of art and good traditions, aficionado of opera and sacred music, and founder of the Sociedad de Amigos del País. He joined the Masons with the pseudonym of Red Eagle, doing a great deal of intense political and philanthropic work, for which he was granted the 33rd degree and given the title of Supreme Inspector Commander. He was the Venerable Master of Eastern Central Lodge No. 13 in Mayagüez, and later Grand National Master, always introducing Masonic and spiritist doctrines into public and private life.

A great deal more has been said about RMC. For example, that he also venerated the Knights Templar, well-known warriors and bankers and devotees of Mary Magdalene, making innumerable pilgrimages to their temples in the motherland. Although the Order of the Temple was persecuted and censored, its Grand Master burned at the stake, and many of its knights martyred by Pope Clement V, it continues to carry out its mission clandestinely. There he was educated by monks devoted to the tradition of Janus, and devoted furthermore to the Black Virgin, goddess of the Earth. Consequently, RMC is a spirit in great demand, since he is invoked by lodges, secret societies, legislators, bankers and investors, government officials and bureaucrats, besides the unemployed, workers, maids, whores, and political exiles.

"RMC, tell me, when will I return to my country? When will I see my wife and children? When will my enemies leave me in peace? When should we hide? When should we come out of hiding?"

2

In order to give the readers an idea of the seriousness of this temple, I should include in my telling the transcript of an interview with doña Clotilde Suárez Moczó, the wife of a very prominent senator. Doña Clotilde was from the Alto de Cangrejos. Her parents arrived from the Balearic Islands without a peseta to their name and through a great deal of effort opened a bakery in downtown San Juan. Doña Clotilde was raised according to the teachings of the Catholic Church, with a great fear of God. She would visit my grandparents' house, sit discreetly in the back of the room, and listen fervently to the spiritist dialogue while holding her rosary in her right hand. Doña Clotilde has graciously consented to take the time to be interviewed. The interview was short, but to the point:

> "To the north of the Alto del Olimpo there was a little hospital, one of the ones that the government opens with red and blue ribbons. Two women in labor lost their babies, and the priest of the Church of Cangrejos was present. That's how the priest was: he never let a chance go by to lavish attention on his

parishioners. In the face of the loss of a loved one, he would spend at least an hour consoling those left behind. He would send a nun or altar boy to parties for birthdays, baptisms, weddings, and anniversaries to celebrate the happy event.

"His sermons at Mass were never anything spectacular—we could even say that sometimes they were incoherent—but the people of the neighborhood understood that this was due to our lack of understanding of divine affairs. Out of all his obligations and duties, what he most enjoyed was working with the children of the parish. That activity he engaged in rather frequently.

"If you counted up all the parishioners of the Church of Cangrejos, altogether there would be less than a hundred, rich and poor. Every Sunday, religiously, we would parti-cipate in Sunday Mass without asking questions. Without wondering who was this new interim priest who was suddenly celebrating Mass here. We took communion and gave thanks for the wooden altar that one of the artisans in the neighborhood had recently made. After Mass we went out to the back patio to drink lemonade made from the rectory's lemon tree. No one dared to ask outright, although some commented in low voices about the absence of our regular priest. Six Sundays passed, and six interim priests shared lemonade over ice.

"One afternoon we got a visit from the secretary to the bishop of San Juan. To our consternation, he informed us that our priest had been declared incompetent by the diocese and was spending some time in the facility for the mentally ill in Mayagüez. We were told that he had attempted suicide upon learning that his brother had borrowed his car, a black Plymouth, and committed a violent crime in it. The bloodstains were still soaked into the vehicle's carpeting. This situation had caused our priest a nervous breakdown from which he had been unable to recover. The secretary asked for our discretion and continued sending interim priests to our parish.

"Lemon season ended, and the mango trees were bursting with fruit. The whispers about our priest and his delicate health intensified as we ate mango cake every Sunday. One intensely hot afternoon, a news bulletin on the radio informed the populace that the priest of the Iglesia de San Mateo had committed suicide. I was making lemonade with the few lemons left in the rectory, and as I was squeezing the pulp from the fruit, and I heard the news. The police, investigating a crime committed in the priest's car, had found a dozen photos of naked children. The police report indicated that this had been his second suicide attempt.

"The Bishop of San Juan came to visit our parish and said he was deeply distressed by the unexpected death of his brother in the priesthood. Once a priest, always a priest, we thought, and began to question our children. From that day forward, I lost all faith in priests and often visited the spiritist temple. Everything the spiritists do is onstage in front of you, and they don't hide in dark rooms with our children" (Tape 1, Side A).

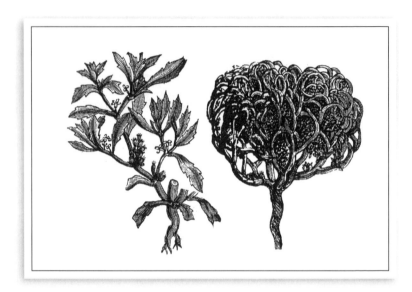

Everyone pay attention to the prayer that will begin momentarily.

PRAYER TO THE ROSE OF JERICHO

*Divine Rose of Jericho, by the blessing that you received
from our Lord Jesus Christ, by the virtue you hold
and the powers granted to you, help me to overcome
the difficulties in my life; give me health, strength, happiness,
serenity, peace in my home, luck in business, skill in my work
to earn more than enough money to take care of all my needs
and those of my home and my whole family.
Divine Rose of Jericho, I ask you all this by the virtue you hold,
in love for Christ Jesus and His great mercy. Amen.*

3

he purpose of the bill is to grant the status of permanent
residence to 150 Galician workers. The bill provides for the
appropriate deductions and for the payment of the required head
taxes and visa fees.]

"¡Qué va, chica! That's the way it's always been. They give permanent status to everybody: Venezuelans, Spaniards, Dominicans,
Cubans, Haitians. NO! NOT Haitians because they're black. There
are enough of them here already."

"Shhhh!" Pilar whispered, contemplating the shroud of night
from one of the armchairs near the window. The moon was hidden behind the mahogany tree and the fluttering of bats' wings
could be heard, altering the outlines of the branches. The air carried the sound of a night bird, which could be made out over the
noise of the chairs, the movement of shoes going up and down the
stairs, and the murmurs of people in the temple. It was Pilar who,
nervous, remained waiting for the spirit of Eusapia Palladino to
manifest herself.

"Comadre, what happened to you in your house was a curse from a spirit made crazy by the heat. Incense and candles to clean out the atmosphere of that home. An incense holder full up with incense and myrrh and candles, make sure they're from a botánica that makes things for Mesa Blanca, none of that other witchcraft, and to protect yourself, take baths in white flowers with a strong smell, letting them sit for seven days. That way you'll be all protected. Don't forget some prayers to ever'one you can. Comadre, the heart of the case is that the spiritual trials of your material life are not over, but you should bear up well, because the trials will help you in your spiritual progress."

"All this stuff about trials is nothing but lies; if some other misfortune befalls my family, just out of plain anger I'll fall into my coffin, flattened by rage. Enough suffering already," Pilar answered.

"Rebellion will do you no good, my girl. It fills you up with anxiety and weighs you down and holds back the development of your soul," Abuelo Juan murmured in her ear.

"Calma, calma, mucha calma, muchacha," Abuela María emphasized.

"How much more calm do you want me to be? Wait patiently for a cement truck to crush the few hopes I have left?"

Pilar is my mother, one of the many curious women in the neighborhood who stopped by to listen to what the spirits had to say. Her mother, old Francisca, passed away when Pilar was little. Francisca hurrying along with a basket of clean clothes balanced on her head along the shoulder of the highway. She walked, furious, bitter, retracing her steps to the house after a run-in with Siete Varas la Gallega. Abuela Francisca lived and died after a lifetime of putting up with the humiliations of Siete Varas, Abuelo Cristóbal's lover. Maybe that was one of her reasons for not having any more children for him, filling her crack with boiled blue nightshade leaves every time he climbed on top of her. Nightshade leaves are good for preventing pregnancy and alleviating the sweats of menopause. For this reason, you will always find that plant in the

Caño and in the yards outside the houses of Concha la Tetona, Siete Varas la Gallega, Lula la Ojos, and Madame Chloë the Haitian. In order to make up for the money that Siete Varas got out of Abuelo Cristóbal, Abuela Francisca put a clandestine lottery in the kitchen, and as she ironed she took care of the numbers business, until one day the Insular Police came and took her away on charges of running an illegal lottery.

"Impossible! My wife is an upright, law-abiding woman," Abuelo Cristóbal exclaimed as he shoved a couple of bills into the sergeant's pocket.

Siete Varas lived in Seboruco, a neighborhood at the edge of one of the mangrove swamps of the Caño, and wore wide skirts with petticoats underneath. With a solid body, narrow hips, a wide back, and her mischievous gaze, no one knows how she ended up in that neighborhood, together with a bunch of vulgar Galicians who would sing fandanguillos over the Caño at night:

> No hay árbol como el nogal
> ni fruta como el madroño,
> ni cuña que ajuste más
> que lo que yo sé del coño
> ¡Ay salero, ay salero, ay salero!
> con el coño se gana el dinero.

"Hey, kid, is your mami around?" Siete Varas interrogated little Pilar one day. The girl, completely naked, was washing herself in the stream of water that flowed through the tin gutters down from the roof of the house.

"Yes, I'm here, and don't you even look at my girl, you'll fill her with your chaos and your evil filth just by looking at her. And in case you don't get it, I don't want to see you around this house again. You, with your skirts all filthy from so many men jumping on you!" Abuela Francisca shouted at her from the balcony.

"Hold your tongue, you vile little woman! I've come to tell you something you already know, something I just wanted to remind you of. Your husband is mine, whether you like it or not!"

"You can keep my husband; what do I care? But the money he earns belongs to this house! I want that to be perfectly clear!"

It was known that Siete Varas practiced witchcraft and was the lover of the Man with the Cloven Hoof. The fan she always carried held the substance of happiness. In the afternoon she would go to Abuelo Cristóbal's store on the pretext of buying root vegetables.

There she flirted with him over and over until she snared him and took him to her house. That was where Abuela Francisca had to go, to the fetid Caño between the pieces of slabs of rotten wood to collect the money he had made at the store before Siete Varas could waste it with the women from her house. She showed up there dressed in white because Abuela Francisca always dressed in white, so that she could not be confused with the unkempt, ragged old women who lived in the Caño or with the women who worked in the houses of Concha la Tetona, Siete Varas la Gallega, Lula la Ojos, and Madame Chloë the Haitian.

"Give me this week's money, Cristóbal. I won't let my daughter go hungry!" Abuela Francisca shouted.

"Get out of my house, machorra, or I'm going to kill you with a whip siete varas de largo!"

It was a hot afternoon and a desert dust cloud had filled the air, decreasing visibility. Abuela Francisca, in a bad mood, went straight to the highway. A truck approached, and even though the driver blew the horn, BAM!!! it ran her over. Her entrails were strewn over the gravel road, and her soul picked them up, piled them back into her body, and traced a tranquil smile on her face. There in the clouds she lived with Fabián, who took her to live a transparent life in a house painted in the clouds. Fabián keeps her so busy that she has no time to spend thinking of the living, although from time to time she escapes from him. Pilar was left motherless; thankfully, old Francisca had taught her the trade of a laundress.

But that's not all that happened to Pilar. One last event came to upset the girl's life even further. She also witnessed the hurricane that flattened the little vegetable shop that belonged to her father, Abuelo Cristóbal, and carried away the cookie tin that held their savings, destroyed the kiosk, and threw the vegetables in all directions. All that was left of the business were the roosters being raised for sale, which were miraculously saved from the winds because her father opened the cages and all the roosters flew to the cave in the mangrove swamp. After the hurricane, Abuelo Cristóbal rolled up the legs of his pants and stuck his feet in a nearby lagoon, letting the fish nibble at his few remaining hopes. Siete Varas was so happy when Abuela Francisca underwent her spiritual change, losing her soul to the limbo of tragic death, but Abuelo Cristóbal estaba triste, tristísimo, and had already lost interest in women. Even so, Siete Varas did not lose hope, and when Abuelo Cristóbal lost his business, she introduced him to a friend of hers from Galicia who dealt in the black market of merchandise, meat, and foodstuffs, and Abuelo Cristóbal didn't think twice. Even so, he paid no attention to the Galician woman, although it should be mentioned that he did learn all kinds of tricks for dealing with the black market trade.

Desperate, the Galician woman went to consult the Haitians who lived in the Caño, and they inundated her with instructions for attracting depressed lovers, broken hearts, and listless souls. She spent the nights serenading water, cutting geraniums and daisies so that at the first light of day she could bathe in water that had been blessed by the moon and sprinkled with flower petals. One night, Abuela Francisca appeared to her in a dream, riding a bicycle. On her head she wore fruit piled into a transparent basket and Siete Varas awoke furious and shivering when Abuela Francisca shouted to her from Heaven, "Your problem is that that merchandise belongs to me!"

Siete Varas got como agua pa' chocolate, drank a swallow of coffee, put on all her petticoats and necklaces, and went out to consult one of the old women of the Caño.

"Morning," Siete Varas said.

"To you too," a sick, toothless, camphor-smelling old woman replied.

"I'm distressed and distraught. My man doesn't want anything to do with me; it's all his wife's fault and there's nothing I haven't tried. And if that weren't enough, that woman appeared to me in a dream riding a bicycle."

That was enough for the old woman to prepare her a recipe for love powders and perfume made of basil and anamú, to which she should add a few drops of menstrual blood and anoint her fan and all her petticoats. She also prescribed essence of Spanish fly, enchanted buttons sewn to the sleeves of her blouse, needles tied with black thread, lianas with seven knots, and belts of garlic and rue that she should hang at midnight around Abuelo Cristóbal's house.

"Why so much stuff?"

"To protect you from the dead woman who appeared in your dream."

"And the Rose of Jericho?"

"It's no good for this kind of thing."

"Then what is the Rose of Jericho good for?"

5

When Pilar's body started to round out and her pubic hair sprouted, she got a job selling notions in the junk shop belonging to Mr. Gautier, the husband of the mayor of San Juan. You don't know what notions are? Let's see, a bit of culture here. "Notions" in business slang means: thread, pins, needles, cosmetics, jewelry, baby clothes, stockings, undergarments, pots, knives, forks, sheets, pillowcases, blankets, toys, et cetera. Working as a clerk was more agreeable than going to collect dirty clothing from the houses of the rich hidalgos of Miramar and dragging sacks of crap-filled shorts, blankets stained with the blood of the daughters of the houses, and shit from the diapers of the little children to the laundresses' district. Washing alien clothing by hand in a big tub with a bar of soap, rinsing, laying out in the sun, wringing and hanging on the barbed wire: all in all it was a contemptible job.

With time, food, and Abuelo Cristóbal's affection, Pilar became a smart, efficient woman. She kept the house in perfect order, took care of Abuelo Cristóbal, shaved him, combed his hair, kept his shirts starched and bleached. She cooked, sewed, cleaned, mopped, and did the dishes, and when Abuelo Cristóbal had to go away on business, she packed him a bag with a change of clothing and a lunchbox with his favorite foods. Abuelo Cristóbal trusted completely in his daughter Pilar because she was absolutely organized and precise, not just at home but also in her studies, which she never abandoned, finishing her high school diploma. In order to forget so much suffering, one day Abuelo Cristóbal said to her, "Mija, go out and have fun on Saturdays," and Pilar took his advice.

Pilar was very pretty indeed, with a mane of black hair that fell to her shoulders and an aquiline nose like those of the Andalusian girls in Granada. Although the most impressive thing about her was not her height, but the steady gaze of her clear black eyes.

Pilar would go out with her coworkers down to the shacks made of palm and yagua branches on the coast, which belonged to the blacks who lived along the beach. In order to defray the costs of her outfits, she would participate in the dance contests, which were fairly popular and a quick way for anyone to earn money. Pilar would dress in reasonably-priced satin and tulle and adorn her body with discount costume jewelry that she found in the big warehouse stores owned by the Majorcans in San Juan. At the dances, she ran away with all the prizes, and people came to know her as one of the best dancers in the area. [Mueve tu fondillo mi negra, que pa'eso te lo dieron.] In the early hours of the morning, she would get into someone's broken-down old car and go down to Loíza, where the blacks ran a rowboat to cross the river. At the yagua shacks along the path, they bought rum and ice and she lay down on the banks of the river so that the breeze cleared her mind. Pilar understood that the physical body must be fed and touched gently so that it doesn't die before its time. You have to sing to it, Quiéreme otra vez, bésame otra vez, como en aquella noche, vuelve a ser de nuevo, brillante arabesco de amor en la noche azul, and while you sing you have to move it slowly, first the feet, without lifting them from the ground, now the hips, just the hips. Así.

6

[Listen to my advice. To make someone love you, all you have to do is write the person's name on a blank piece of paper with your own blood. Wear the paper for a month on the left side of the chest.] The third time that Pilar visited the temple, she sat in one of the armchairs and looked toward the back of the house. There was a murmur of voices in the parlor, different from the laughter and many voices in the kitchen, especially a man's voice. Felipe was telling his sisters about the beginning of the authorities' cleaning of the Caño. Minerva and Claudia Luz were washing the supper dishes, Cecilia was fixing Carmen's hair, and Fernando was looking out the window at the birds sitting on the branches of the mahogany tree. Pilar got out of her chair and asked where the bathroom was. Abuela María pointed toward the back of the house and half a second later Pilar was in front of Felipe. Fernando kept watching the birds; Minerva and Claudia Luz glanced up for two seconds; Cecilia and Carmen didn't even notice. Claudia Luz detected a flirtatious spark in Felipe's eyes, Minerva observed how Pilar was devouring that fine body with her eyes, while Felipe continued his monologue about street improvements and the construction of sewers. "This is what they mean by 'progress we're all going to enjoy in some way.'"

Felipe was fascinated by the substance of things. The substance that moves the women who pass by on the sidewalk in front of his house and the substance contained in the hips of the female parishioners at the parlor. The substance of late-model convertibles. The substance of a cement house with a carport and balcony. The substance of linen clothing decorated in silk. The substance of baby-doll nightgowns, good tobacco, and seductive perfume. The substance that will control progress on the island and which will fill this territory with highways and new housing. The substance that the U.S. dollar is made from. The particular substance that will allow him to have a good job, spend money on women, and provide for his family; the substance of the black-haired, black-eyed woman standing in front of him. And I believe, and have seen it proven over and over, en la cárcel y en la cama se conocen los amigos, that's all you need, this dish needs salt and I'm the one to season it. [¡Mete mano, Felipín!]

"I've met a wonderful man. He's amazing. The only problem is that he seems to be a player," Pilar confided to her friend Bella.

"You can do it," Bella answered.

Pilar first saw Bella on the patio of a coffee shop called El Rancho Azul, long before she began dreaming of having the type of family that she saw every day in newspaper photos. There, posed for the benefit of our San Juan society, was the perfect family: three precious children, the always-elegant wife, the provider-husband. They were people who married for life and had a yard full of bougainvilleas. Everyone would sit down at the table and chat about how their day had been.

Bella was as tall as the old pine trees along the coast, with a well-formed body, perfect nose and mouth, and a shining mane of black hair. She was a woman who attracted men naturally. She completed the requirements to be a sewing teacher and looked without success for a job until through sheer luck she found a position as a clerk in the same store where Pilar worked. Bella was a poet and wrote poems to la patria and a long-lost love, which is the same thing. She wrote poetry and organized it into manuscripts, which she printed in small quantities at Imprenta Venezuela, which was owned by the Widow Morales. The Widow Morales, when she saw the effort the young woman put into being published, allowed her to pay by installments. "Pay me whenever you can, but pay me," the Widow Morales would repeat.

Bella used her lunch hours to place her book of poetry in drugstores and newsstands in Old San Juan. On weekends she would take a public car and go to small towns to place her book at different businesses, and at night she could often be seen at meetings of sugar-cane workers and protests of the drivers of public transportation. In time she met the poets of island society and began to be invited to their salons. When she made her entrance at the meetings, the gentlemen there would turn to see her beauty; after all, las canas, los cuernos y la borrachez no vienen por vejez. The gazes, the pure flirtation and the compliments ended, most of the time, in a horizontal acquaintance with the body's needs.

Pilar loved to share everything, small or great, with Bella, whom she saw as an old friend, a comrade in the same battle. She read Bella's poetry and understood every word, the way one understands the circle and the horizon, with the satisfaction of always having known. Pilar felt that reason would leave her every time she met up with Bella, and together they would go through Rimbaud's dark halls, the ringing of Neruda's bells, and the peace of Mistral's landscape. Pilar loved Bella from the moment they met, the way she also loved Felipe; but Bella wanted to throw herself into the world with open arms, with her poetry and everything. She wanted to explore different seas, bodies with varied temperatures, other climates of bread. Words were her ally, but within the censorious island circle, a one letter could cause many catastrophes. The police machine exploded with fury at a word, a badly phrased or wrongly written sentence, to say nothing of poetry, because poetry is a creature of double meanings.

"Come on, Bella, tell me what you've written lately. Read me your poems out loud."

"Pilarcita, you know one can't speak out loud. This country is very small. Everyone knows everyone."

"All right, then, let's go to a dark, secluded place amidst the palm trees, and the sound of the surf will serve as a protective wall." And so they went. To any hut made of yagua branches along the coast, to drink rum with crushed ice and coconut milk, to laugh at the antics of the dozens of children who would come to the table hoping for a few coins. Sometimes they walked up to El Morro, to the tip of the structure, to see how the walls held back the waves and the colonies of sea urchins flourished in big black cocoons.

One Sunday afternoon, while they were hanging out in sandy little Muñoz Rivera Park under those large trees, Pilar confessed to Bella, "I told you about Felipe the other day. I'm still thinking about him. His sarcastic gaze, that fine mulato body, me tienen mal. Besides, I'd like to get married. I'd like to have a family. I can't spend my whole life flitting from man to man, and I think Felipe is the one."

"Sounds great to me," Bella answered while pulling a flask of rum out of her bag. She opened the bottle and poured a shot of the liquid, gave it to Pilar to sip, and then drank the rest. Now they were walking toward the little museum of stuffed and mounted animals. When the door opened, the atmosphere was filled with a smell of old resin and alcohol. The figures of the animals posed majestically on the walls with their old glass eyes. The darkness of the site allowed for a gentle caress.

"Good, good, compadre Felipillo. This one is good for you. I'll take this one for you," Eusapia Palladino announced. The grandparents exchanged looks, and Pilar and Felipe hugged. The table cleared. The tablecloth shifted, eight cups of wine and a jar of olives tipped over. At that moment creaking was heard. One of the mediums began to speak in tongues. A strong smell of blue coal and a silence beyond all silences came over the room. Pilar began to fan herself with her fan with black ribs. The spirit spoke: "I am very old; I think I have been old all my life. When he disappears, a tremble runs through my whole body, slight but constant. Abandonment. The muscles of my shoulders tighten, my heart beats faster, and my whole body becomes alert. That's when I age more."

"You're not a woman anymore," Abuelo Juan answered. "You're an ethereal being that wanders through the atmosphere, and you have no sex."

"What do *you* know about what a spirit is?" the tormented soul exclaimed. "I imagine him in another bed and I'm beside myself. I need him like a Siamese twin needs his other half, and I wait for him, I wait for him until the wee hours of the morning when he arrives, often drunk on rum, with a happy spirit. Tired. I don't know how many times I've seen him licking another woman's body, taking her in a different way, even tearing her apart. I spy on him between one beer and another. His head spins in a great sexual fever, and deep down he didn't want to penetrate her, but rather all of them together and me as well. His bestiality has no limits, but neither do his limitations. That's why I insist and mount him as many times as I feel like!"

Abuelo Juan gave instructions that anyone who was under-age should leave the parlor, and then focused on confronting this spirit with all the force of an enemy. "I insist that you remember your spiritual nature. He is alive and you are already dead. The ties that bound you together have disappeared. He doesn't owe anything to you, nor do you owe anything to him."

"It's useless for you to keep bellowing, you dirty old man. It's useless; he's missing, and the worst part is that he has my identity in his pocket. Tell him to give me back what's mine and I'll leave him alone immediately!" the spirit shouted.

Despite all his knowledge and his morals and ethics, Abuelo Juan lost his temper and began to hurl insult after insult without understanding that the only thing wrong with that spirit was that she still longed for the love that the living found in bed. Pilar moved her fan so rapidly that the ribs started to come apart. At that moment RMC declared, "Even if you take the necessary precautions, unfortunate things can happen at the mesa blanca. The dark regions of the universe intersect with the heat of these islands, and the invocation can bring spirits that are jokers, mis-chievous, unable to deal with the same oxygen as human beings, addicted to the libido and witchcraft. On the other hand, it's vital to understand and respect the hierarchies of spirits. On the first order are the ones who have reached perfection, the pure spirits; on the second, the ones who are in the middle of the scale, the ones who work for the achievement of good; and on the third are the imperfect spirits, who are still at the beginning of the scale; their nature is one of ignorance, evil passions, and the wish to do mischief, which delays their progress. Those spirits, inclined to do mischief, are comparable to the work of witches in the material world."

"Cut out the nonsense, compadre, what this is all about is that Felipillo has done his own thing in other lives and now the debris is sticking to him. That little problem, I will stick it in my sack of tribulations and send it flying out into the air. Let's not talk any more about it. Pilar, mi niña, this one is good for you. I'll take this one for you," Eusapia Palladino concluded.

Like a spring, Felipe stood up from his chair and moved toward the balcony, went down the stairs, and announced to the group of guys under the mahogany tree, "Let's get this party started! I declare a week of fun because I'm getting married soon." [And so it was!] While Pilar was completely occupied taking charge of the wedding, the young men of the neighborhood organized an itinerary of nocturnal outings that included stops at all the bars in San Juan, plus the yagua huts on the coast, ending up in the houses of Concha la Tetona, Siete Varas la Gallega, Lula la Ojos, and Madame Chloë the Haitian. In each of these houses, Felipe and his friends went from bed to bed with every friendly mongrel they met. Body to body is all you need to free the emotions from the flesh.

After every nighttime excursion, they would stop for a breakfast of rice with fried eggs and ¡Fuerza-Fuerza! mondongo with chicken broth, because they say it's good for maintaining virility. Then, making as little noise as possible, he would enter his parents' house and collapse into the first bed he found. [Ay, Felipe! Be careful! You don't want to catch something down there, so that afterwards you have to live on memories!]

The day of the wedding, two metal arches covered with baby's breath, gardenias, and carnations decorated the front door of Pilar's house. White balloons, a three-layer cake, and sugar-coated almonds waited on a table like abandoned Buddhas. For those who missed the performance, I report that the bride's silhouette was accented by draped silk crepe with a few strips of tulle around the bodice. Around her neck there hung a delicate chain that closed in front with a brooch made of pearls and semiprecious stones, which Abuelo Cristóbal had acquired from a rich client who owed him money for some meat. Her bouquet of lilies and carnations ran down her skirt with ribbons of baby's breath. Felipe wore an immaculate linen suit with matching shoes and a small bow tie at the neck contrasting with the rest of the outfit. Bella wore a close-fitting red suit with her hair pulled back in a bun, which made it easy to mistake her for a bolero singer from Club Esquife about to sing "Qué falso eres," so the guests were stunned when she recited the following poem:

Little rose
at times tiny and naked,
you fit in one of my hands,
in my temple, in my ear, in my eye
and I can carry you to my mouth, but
you move like a deep breast
a new waist
and my arm does not manage to encircle you
while you open like a great maddened love
and I lean down to leave you.

Felipe, enchanted, applauded, and all the guests imitated him. The couple lost themselves in an embrace and Pilar sobbed with emotion. [¡Qué fiestón!]

Abuelo Cristóbal talked all night with his compadres about raising roosters and his big business while strutting around the room in a Panamanian linen suit. Old Cristóbal had become one of the island's greatest providers. Supervising his business personally, at night he went out in a boat on the high seas to wait for merchandise thrown from airplanes that originated from Venezuela, or else he would come to the coast from Cabo Rojo to wait for oilcloth rucksacks filled with merchandise from Santo Domingo. He knew all the clandestine slaughterhouses in the area and transported their products by wrapping women's bellies with cuts of meat to simulate pregnancy. At Abuelo Cristóbal's request, the seamstresses in the neighborhood sewed skirts with pockets twelve inches long that could be filled with rice, flour, and jewelry. He simulated babies wrapped in blankets, which were really silk bags, and hung rashers of jamón serrano and Manchego cheese on men's backs to make them look like hunchbacks. In the iron pipes and metal cylinders of the cars, he transported pitorro rum, and to the milk that was on sale he added 50 percent water and resold it at the same price. To the few pianos that came to the island, he added a false bottom and inserted silk stockings, evening bags, and perfume bottles filled with pearls, coral, and tortoiseshell. In the coffins that came from the carpenter shops, they transported pigs' feet and codfish stolen from the navy's ships.

Between the neighbors, family, Abuelo Cristóbal's customers, and the temple parishioners, the house was packed to the rafters. Two cooks kept the stove lit with a sancocho and goat fricassee, and Abuela María carried and fetched trays of fried morcillita, sweet and sour peas, and fresh almojábanas. Fernando stuck close to the musicians, serving them drinks and bringing them food. Felipe, with the excuse that he was the groom, passed out squeezes and embraces, dancing with every woman who placed herself in front of him.

"Felipe, I'm going to miss you," a young woman with black eyes said to him.

"Don't miss me, I'm not dead. I'm here whenever you want me, mi negra."

Minerva was seen coming and going from the festivities with all the young people of the neighborhood. Claudia Luz was accompanied by her boyfriend El Gringo, an agronomist she had met on the public bus. In the yard, the old people played dominoes and several girls in brightly-colored skirts walked up and down, packing down the earth with the clicking of their heels. Carmen danced only with Víctor, a soldier who courted her every time he got permission to leave the base, while Cecilia talked all night with her girlfriends from the neighborhood. Bella was seen flirting with Mr. Gautier's son; they were seen in the yard, in the parlor when it started to drizzle, in the hallway leading to the bedrooms, and she was seen collecting her wrap and purse, holding the man's hand. [DID YOU SEE THAT WOMAN? SHE STOLE SOMEONE'S HUSBAND!!!]

9

The dream of my birth made it possible for Pilar to hear the murmur of the wet, refreshing sea. We lived in a tenement of wood houses surrounded by a mango and avocado grove and several fetid swamps full of horned toads, mosquitoes, and blind cockroaches. The hens and their chicks pecked at the sidewalks and when the wind changed suddenly, a smell like a pigsty invaded the atmosphere. Pilar and Felipe were two of the many in a country where work was scarce; drivers and sugarcane workers were continually on strike; children were bursting with ringworm and lice; schools were notable in their lack; the streets were infected with children dedicated to all kinds of mischief and forbidden games; bedbugs wreaked havoc; beggars combed through the rich people's trash in the middle of the night; the jails were full of unfortunates charged with stealing pigs and poultry; and in the houses of Concha la Tetona, Siete Varas la Gallega, Lula la Ojos, and Madame Chloé the Haitian, the whores cleansed their pussies every night as a way to control the crabs. When the authorities picked them up to disinfect them, they jumped over the walls of the clinics and went back to the bordellos. Perfumes, textiles, shoes, and accessories were in short supply; many families survived on cornmeal and plátanos sancochaos, since there was no rice, lard, meat, or sugar to put on the table.

To top it all off, a group of nationalists, led by a man that everyone called don Pedro, called for a national uprising: "I advise women to make their homes a sanctuary for pure, brave men, those who love liberty; and I call on all Puerto Ricans to arm themselves with revolvers, rifles, pistols, shotguns, knives, machetes, whips, dirks, daggers, and anything they can find to defend the cause of la Revolución," he announced one day on a radio station.

Pilar heard this news while I was at her breast, without understanding the madness that was invading the whole country. Pilar declared, "It's about inventing happiness for yourself; it's about getting along with the neighbors; it's about having a husband you love at home; it's about having a few babies for him; it's about buying your own home; it's about having a well-kept garden; it's about rice, lard, and sugar appearing."

Pilar was answering the radio while I sucked and sucked furiously, because her body had become tense and the milk wasn't coming naturally, and I began to bawl until I tired myself out and Pilar realized that there was a baby hanging from her breast and the neighbor-woman stuck her head in the window and called "Pilar, would you like some linden tea?"

"I don't need your infusions."

And I started to bawl again because by now Pilar had become as tense as a broom belonging to one of the witches of the Caño. I know that we must be careful, because the spirits do not have powers equal to those of the old women who disguise themselves as handsome men and well-behaved children and chop people up and take them into the mangrove swamp to eat them.

I was sucking and sucking while I listened to the neighbor's story because she talked so loudly that the whole neighborhood could hear what she was saying: "Haven't you seen the Aparecido?"

"What are you talking about?"

"That thing that floats along the paths and goes into your house, but not through the doors or the windows. You're bathing, and when you get out of the shower and are just putting on your panties, suddenly there he is. You feel him, but you can't see him. Women who have been able to see him say he's mulato, with green eyes and a great body, more handsome than don Pedro; and they say don Pedro is very handsome and drives all the women crazy."

"What do I care about stories about apparitions and agitators? I have a daughter to feed and I have to give thanks for the husband I have found, for his eyes like a tiger's, for his man's smell, for his warmth, for his sobriety and also for his drunkenness, for my happiness, for the nights he comes home early and goes to the kitchen to make dinner while I break my back cleaning his clothes in the washtub on the patio. Thank you for the habichuelas espesas you make, macho mío; it's fine for me to wash your perfumed shorts; thank you for the sofrito that you stir that smells like ham and bacon; thank you for calling, 'Baby, dinner is ready. Don't forget that I need two shirts starched and ironed for tomorrow,' and thank you for coming to my arms, to our bed for me to take care of you when you're drunk. Ay, Felipe, I ask you to be careful, where have you been, with who, why are you home so late, why is there lipstick on your shirt; but it doesn't matter because I must give thanks for this house; even if it falls to dust, it protects us from the elements, and I give thanks because I'm married and that's what counts."

10

The entire country began to play the lottery as a way to escape poverty, and Felipe was no exception. Thus he hit the jackpot and bought his first car. It was a Plymouth with a broken radio, five years old, that had belonged to a priest from the Church of San Mateo. It was late at night when Felipe said goodbye to Pilar to go out for a spin with his friends. About midnight, Pilar was awoken by the neighbor-woman's shouting. Felipe had been arrested as a suspect. His car was identical to the one the nationalists had used to transport two loaded .38-caliber pistols, five bombs, hundreds of bullets, and a submachine gun. The neighbor gave Pilar some tea and swallowed a pill that the doctor had prescribed for her.

"What's that?" Pilar asked.

"It's for nerves, mija."

"Let me have one, too."

At the Insular Police on Calle San Francisco, the line of people arrested already stretched around the block. The whole country was a suspect, and Felipe was no exception.

"A police patrol stopped me, approached, and told me not to take another step just as I heard the bullets crackling. There was a torrential downpour and everyone had to run for shelter, including the police patrol. I dodged the bullets until I managed to duck into a nearby house. A detective entered with his gun in his hand and took me out to the street. Twenty-five feet away was the National Guard with shotguns and machine guns. 'Put your hands up,' one said. 'What we should do is shoot him,' another said.

"They dragged me to a truck full of people and took the car away. On the way to the police station, I saw men and women crouched behind posts, lying face-down under cars and under houses, on the roofs, behind Dumpsters. I saw people shielding themselves with sheets of tin and hiding from bullets behind trees. I saw a man who lit a sock on fire and threw it at a patrol car. At the Insular Police, I saw women who were almost naked and thought what a fucking mess I'd gotten myself into when I bought that car."

It would be a long time before Felipe would use the Plymouth again. The car was returned in awful condition, and for a long time it shone in the dark yard like a giant beetle. Felipe washed it every Saturday, went for a spin around the neighborhood, and put it back in the rear of the yard as if it were an elephant in the parlor. I didn't like to look out the window at night because I would be faced with the immensity of that beetle, and cry until Pilar came in and closed the window. Then I would curl up on my cot and my sleep would deepen and a tall man would approach my tiny bed and tell me things without moving his lips, and a chorus of brilliant fireflies, like stars about to burst, would spin and spin through the air in my room and with their arms that are not really arms push the man who is not really a man, who is an Aparecido, who is a witch from the Caño, an old woman like a soul in torment smiles and I can't dream anymore and I scream for a long time and Felipe picks me up in his arms and carries me to the bed and we all sleep together: Felipe, Pilar, and me.

Early one morning Pilar went out with me on her shoulder. She went to the grandparents' house to have me blessed, for them to give me a spiritual bath, to put me in a washbasin filled with holy water, to get mi abuela María's blessing, to give me a hand made of jet, to have prayers said over me. My grandparents took off my clothes and wrapped me in a white sheet. Tía Minerva approached and gave me a kiss. Everyone had to wait while Abuela María heated water and put it in a silver-colored brass basin. By then my grandmother was speaking in tongues.

Pilar grabbed me around the body, almost breaking my head open as she put me in the silver-colored basin. Tía Minerva began to throw tepid water on me with a big wooden spoon. Abuelo Juan, his anger fiery, cursed the spirits who had dared to disturb his granddaughter's peace, and what everyone was expecting, happened. That spirit flew in. He floated through the bathroom curtain. I didn't cry, but waited for him to notice me. The spirit smiled, and I smiled, and my grandfather took the broom and pulled the curtain down. The spirit, without moving his lips, told me not to be afraid, and I smiled again, and the spirit blew a kiss toward my forehead, and I closed my eyes. A chorus of fireflies appeared, surrounding the apparition in a circle of light, disappearing in the act.

"Look, compadre Juan, remember that this is a spirit in torment, an errant soul that doesn't understand the separation of the body from the soul; those hot flashes he's causing you aren't good. With these spirits you have to be really prepared. And remember that they give in more than we do. Soon enough I'm going to throw him into my sack of problems, but not for long, because these spirits know how to escape from traps. The problem with the baby girl is that this character was her master in another life and he doesn't understand that the gig is up. With possessive spirits like that, you have to have a lot of patience, because they can take control of any substance when they feel like it. A lot of prayer, and put white flowers in the girl's room. White flowers

will help to cleanse the girl's aura and that tormented soul will
go away."

Abuela María unscrewed the top of the bottle of Agua Florida
and flicked the water into the air with the tips of her fingers, and
at that moment Abuelo Juan's posture began to straighten up; he
raised his head and his arms moved to an elegant, serene position
like a king addressing his entourage.

"Certain types of spirits follow Satan; they let themselves be
seduced by ghosts and the Devil's illusions. They believe that late
at night they can fly like pagan gods, and in those silent hours
they rise up and attack the small, the sick, the invalids; they have
the same effect as the witches." It was RMC speaking.

"This bullshit doesn't convince me," my mother said.

One Saturday afternoon, Pilar took me with my bottle and everything else and set off by herself down the path. The neighbor,
suspecting where she was going, called, "Pilar, do you want me
to go with you?"

"No, thanks." Pilar headed off down the gravel road with me
in her arms until she entered the labyrinth of the Caño.

"Where do the old women live?"

"Over that way," That One said, gesturing with his arm.

The old women were gathered together, crouched down at
the entrance to the Caño, smoking tobacco and drinking malt
alcohol because it's good for the blood, and Pilar asked, "Which
one of you will help me?"

"Any of us," one of them answered.

And all of them got up and went into a shack that smelled of
alcohol. One moved aside the yagua branches so that air could
come in through a crack in the wall, another lit an oil lamp to
provide some light, and a third sat down on the floor to listen to
Pilar's story. When Pilar told them about the Aparecido, one of

the old women put me on the dirt floor in the center of a circle of river pebbles. There each of the three cut a piece from the fabric of her clothing with a knife that had been stabbed into the ground in a corner of the shack. With the same knife, one of them moved away, took a dove from a cage, and with one stroke cut off its head and put its body next to the pieces of fabric. I played with the centipedes that sprouted from the earth. Pilar sat near the circle, watching. One of the old women left the hut and walked to the bank of the Caño. She stuck out her tongue and moved it repeatedly, producing a squeaking sound like a hungry rat, while the other two witches tore apart a piece of local lettuce and chewed it fiercely. The old woman shouted over the dark water of the Caño, "This is the sacrifice we're making for you, señol de la na', leave this soul alone! What young woman can we get fer yeh to give yeh some pleasure? Tell us her shape, her smell, the perfume of her blood, so we can get her fer yeh."

[Of course, the present situation has developed because of an increasing growth in population with no land frontier to be pushed forward and with an insufficiently rapid increase in productivity.]

"Don't trust no one, look people straight in the eye. Everyone's walking 'round scared. The fuzz is out all night combing the streets and there are whistle-blowers everywhere. Be careful what you say, where you go, who you talk to. Be careful; don't let nothin' happen to you. Don Pedro's war's begun."

"What a man he is!"

"All by himself, shooting it out with the Insular Police. That man has sure got balls. But the problem is there ain't many of them. They're going to beat them to a pulp."

"Last night I was out that way visiting one of my cousins. He's one of the soldiers patrolling the Palace of Santa Catalina."

"And? So what's up?"

[Palomilla, palomilla tu historia es muy importante, te acusan de criminal y no has matado a nadie.] On the corner a group of men talk in low voices, while cars go up and down in lines along the streets, roads, and boulevards; stray dogs sniff each others' asses; and cockroaches make a mad dash for the nearest sewer. Old women dressed in white, with their black parasols to shade themselves from the sun, walk hurriedly between the alleyways, bodegas, small businesses, school supply stores, movie theaters, and schools. Without stopping, everyone says hello, shakes hands, says "Good afternoon," the men looking for something to do, but there's nothing because jobs are scarce and there's no work to be done and they get tired of coming and going until they stop on the corner underneath that mahogany tree to spy on what the old women are doing; in the middle of the noise: people talking, radios, car engines, buses, who is that woman with the little girl? I don't know pero está buenísima, while the breeze tangles in the branches of the trees and This One brings out his bongo drums and That One begins to sing and the Other comes out sleepily onto the balcony to enjoy the duo, who end up waking the children from their afternoon siesta.

"If they don't get some help down there, they're going to get lynched."

"Quiet, they can hear you! Remember, on this island, the most common animal is the rat."

In the backyard the roosters crow, shut up in their cages, and the women move the clothes from the washtubs of their love to the sun of their sadness, thinking, What can I cook tonight without rice, sugar, or lard, besides corn flour and plátanos sancochaos?, praying that the soneo won't wake up the little ones, and that they'll have time to soak the beans for tomorrow and desalt the codfish and soak the laundry for that good-for-nothing man who hasn't been back in a week, because he said he has to go to Ponce to work, that it's the only job he's been able to get and the transportation is bad, all that up and down the mountains makes him vomit up even the lining of his entrails, I hope I have time to listen to the radio soap opera that's so good and also to drink a buchecito of coffee.

On the corner underneath the mahogany tree, three beats on the conga and a movement of the body, two beats like that, and the rhythm repeats until the euphoria of its beat flows through the

very fiber of your spirit, while don Pedro shoots it out with the boys
from the National Guard and even with the governor himself.
[Eso sí que daba pena.] Knock off the bullshit, don Pedro! but
he looks so good in the newspapers; he's always surrounded by
women looking at him like he was a saint come down from Heav-
en, enjoying the war so much, with his muscles so strong, his male
member so appealing. Who would've thought that from waiting
for my husband for so long that I would end up spying on crinkly-
haired chests, but with balls to make your bladder burst, because
I believe the governor doesn't have nearly the balls that that guy
has and that's why he decided to do away with the poor man, but
the governor also has his charm, I like what he says and I'm going
to support him to see if he can bring some progress to this little
island and those layabouts on the corner will get jobs and give up
their damned soneo every afternoon, and rice, lard, and sugar will
appear and that good-for-nothing will get a job closer to home.

In a corner of the living room I remember Pilar curling up in an
armchair, turning on the lamp, and opening the newspaper. I
would lie at her side while I fixed my doll's hair. And the truth is
that there was very little that Pilar could read in the newspaper,
since in order to take care of the whole business with don Pedro
once and for all, the governor proceeded to pass a law about official
secrets, which established that correspondence would be inter-
cepted, telephone calls monitored, and government files sealed.
Furthermore, he organized a secret commission with broad powers to question any movement, conversation, or neighborly visit,
and he sent all the students and workers suspected of being don
Pedro's henchmen to jail. Just in case, the naval war fleet placed
submarines with high-powered radar all around the territory,
including distant crags; and mountainous regions were combed
by tall blond boys bursting with sores from mosquito bites.
    "Well, they're scientists."

"Don't be an idiot! Tanto tiempo en el cercao y no conoces la yerba. You ought to know better by now."

The whole country became one huge whisper, and a silence beyond all silences overpowered everyone. Even so, news spread at the speed of light, circulating among neighbors, friends, co-workers, and family members.

A fist pounding on the door woke Pilar from out of her apathy. Felipe left the bedroom and opened the door.

"The owner of the Plymouth?"

"That's me."

"Can we talk for a moment?"

"Sure."

"What I'm asking you for will sound strange, but we need you to lend us your vehicle."

"I don't lend out what's mine, and that includes my house, my car, and my woman. And by the way, I don't care about the noise you're making. All that matters to me is the dollar. I couldn't care less what government we have. You guys, if you're hungry and want some food, my wife will serve you in the kitchen, but besides that, I don't want to see you around this house again. Pilar, come serve these guys!"

Pilar got out plates and flatware and served arroz con gandules and pork with fried plantains.

"Where did you come from?"

"From far away."

"Are you running away?"

"Absolutely, and they told us that the gentleman with the Plymouth could help us."

"Who told you to come here?"

"Bella Juncos."

"Maybe I can help you."

"If you would let us, the only thing we want is for you to let us examine the Plymouth. There's something we've come looking for."

EXCERPT FROM THE GOVERNOR'S SPEECH

[I've said it before and I'll say it again: this country's got it going on!!!]

"It's not true. There's no problems here. Everything is under control. A few worthless rebels. On this island everything works divinely. Here [if one eats] the number of paved streets, how many children have received free shoes and glasses, [two eat,] how many bottle factories have been erected, [if two eat,] how many hospitals have been built, how many health nurses have joined the battle against parasites and germs, [three eat,] how many agricultural laboratories have been created, how many electrical poles have been put up, [if three eat,] how many pipes for drinking water have been imported, how many automobiles have been imported, [four eat,] and how many telegraph lines cross this territory: that's all I'm saying, what I have said, and what I will continue to declaim with my peace flag against [four eat] this calamity of insults, abuse, assaults, and violence; I repeat what I said, what I've said before, [four eat] which is the need for all of us to eat at the same table, so that you can see with your own eyes that the whole country [four eat] is a huge project of national construction, [four eat] we'll build hotels with private swimming pools and hallways with Murano glass lamps, racetracks with artificial-turf [four eat] tracks, tennis courts, docks for yachts and luxury boats, courses for auto racing, golf courses, [four eat] country clubs with bars and gentlemen's lounges, nightclubs, and casinos. The Pearl of the Antilles [four eat] will become the delight of golfers, beach-lovers, horse- and auto-racers and all this, my dear countrymen, will bring jobs and dollars. They'll build mansions along the shore and luxury automobiles will fill our streets and progress will finally have reached this island that has been cursed for so many years."

12

"¡Óyeme, mi negra, este país está que arde!"

"Who is that talking on the radio?" Pilar asked.

"The governor, mija. Oye, mi negra, listen to the news I have for you!" Felipe announced. "I'm the new manager of communications for the telephone company. My job is to supervise the installation of telephone lines for the whole island. I'll have a late-model car and all the benefits of a high-level executive."

"That sounds marvelous!" And Pilar ran to embrace her husband.

After a three-month training period, Felipe began to travel from town to town. Going into the mountains, ravines, puddles, and fields, he supervised the installation of cables, poles, and wires. Often, in order to check the work of his crew of employees, he would climb up poles, trees, and tobacco warehouses. Night would find him in those mountains, while the local women watched him closely. Tired, he would go to the nearest hole-in-the-wall and fill up on beer. He would spend a long time playing billiards and drinking. The ladies would begin to approach him, and he watched each one's every move like a hawk. They sat with him at a little table in the corner, and when it was time to say good-bye, they would go with him to the nearest hotel, or take him to any one of their beds. When it was time to continue his work in another town, the ladies would roast a suckling pig or party until dawn at one of those holes-in-the-wall. Often he had to return to the town to continue adjusting the telephone facilities, and the ladies, as always, would share their warm, moist beds with him.

In less than five years, Felipe was chosen by the company to serve as a consultant on telephone line installation for several countries in the Caribbean and Central America. He traveled to Colombia, Costa Rica, and Guatemala, and the parade of women did not end. This time they were secretaries, ministry assistants, and paralegals, and all of them served themselves up to him without shame or remorse. Felipe, neither lazy nor shy, would take two or three cunts with him to his hotel every night. Hands and bodies would become a tangle of groans, plunging into a sea of delights. The next day it was "wham, bam, thank you ma'am" and Felipe, always accompanied by army officers, continued on his way as a telephone executive transported in private planes and helicopters, rowboats, motorboats, jeeps, and pickup trucks.

A palo va y a palo viene, passing from one girl to the next, he traveled from one border to another without noticing any difference in the territory, as Mayas, Ladinos, mestizos, whites, blacks, and Asians mixed together, evening out the tourist landscape. In Guatemala he traveled to Petén and to the highlands in the center of the country, the Atlantic seaboard, and the Southern coast, where he encountered cattle, deer, monkeys, peccaries, jaguars, tapirs, pumas, crocodiles in the Polochi River, manatees in Izabal Lake, and of course an infinite variety of quetzals. In Costa Rica, he traveled from Guanacaste to Talamanca, and there was no choice but to walk a good while along the paths leading up in the central cordillera. He made forays into the jungle, machete in hand, trying to find stable land on which to erect telephone poles, and there he met Bribi and Cabecar Indians, who in exchange for rum would offer their virgin women and bunches of plantains. The army would turn over the rum, and the golden bodies of the young women would pass from hand to hand among the crews of workers and soldiers, and naturally to Felipe, who felt no remorse in taking advantage of them.

The trips to Colombia were the ones that Felipe enjoyed most. The government put him up in the best hotels, all expenses paid, and offer him a car and driver at his service twenty-four hours a day. In Bogotá, he made the rounds through all the fashionable cabarets, giving it to all the cigarette girls, waitresses, dancers, and singers. Whenever he had the chance, he would get them on all fours, playing at multiplication tables, and they groaned with pleasure. He traveled from La Guajira to the Ciénaga Grande de Santa María, and when he reached the Bay of Cartagena, it was so comfortable that he felt right at home. In order to go to the Andes with his crew of employees, the government provided a war convoy. From Bucaramanga to the Orinoco River, he felt just like a character out of José Eustasio Rivera's *La vorágine*, since he was always accompanied by anteaters, tapirs, pumas, raccoons, monkeys, and jaguars, which attacked the wheels of the convoy.

Not long afterwards, Felipe landed in Havana, and the government authorities put him up in the famous Havana Riviera, with its patios with fountains, ceramic tiles, ferns, gardenias, and poppies. It was the first of many stays there, since his trips to Havana became more and more frequent. He arrived at the hotel and set out to see the streets, cathedrals, fortresses, and palaces, always at the sides of government officials, all with the purpose of preparing a master plan to erect telephone poles and string lines across the city. With time, Felipe became mature, interesting, refined, and well-acquainted with the great cities of the Caribbean. On Sunday afternoons he would have lunch at Sloppy Joe's, and at night he would usually make the rounds of Sans Souci and El Floridita. He would invite the city's most elegant women to spend the afternoon at the Jockey Club, and at night invite the one he liked best to his room. Meanwhile, he would take the opportunity to give her a tongue bath, and in unison they would do the up and down dance over and over. He met musicians, composers, and announcers for the Cadena Azul radio station, and through Bobby Capó, Tito, and Johnny Rodríguez he met cabaret dancers with exuberant bodies, skin the color of cinnamon, and exotic plumage, whom he managed to nail without shame or glory, twirling them like a cheap nylon stocking and sticking his cock in the place where it hurts least. Whenever he returned to Puerto Rico, he would come with an enviable tan, four cases of the best rum, the most exquisite cigars, linen suits and French perfume for the little woman, Swiss chocolates and Spanish toys for his young daughter, guayaberas cut to fit for Abuelo Juan and Abuelo Cristóbal, Japanese kimonos for his sisters, and a selection of the best records for Fernando. Felipe would take me into his arms and cover me with kisses.

"Nothing like Havana," he would say over and over.

13

Meanwhile, Pilar, on a daily basis, made sure that everything was in order with regard to the running of the house, including her husband's absence. She had long since stopped working in Mr. Gautier's store, since the money Felipe earned was more than enough.

They saved up the down payment for a good cement house with a shining bathroom and kitchen, a terrace, balcony, and carport in one of the new developments built by private investors. It had all the modern conveniences, floors made of the best terrazzo tile and Miami windows of shining glass. The doors to the terrace had double-paned glass, and the bathroom accessories were blue and coordinated with the floor tiles. Pilar would run her hands over the surface of those tiles, admiring the perfection of their design.

To distract herself, she decided to take classes in pastry making offered to housewives by the Extensión Agrícola. She learned to make turroncitos de chocolate, mantecaditos, flan with syrup, and rellenos de crema. She beat eggs, mixed jams and flour, and heated the syrup for the flan slowly until she got bored of so much toffee-making. I would go to the kitchen with my notebook and pencil, and copy down recipes to take to the next Future Home-makers meeting at school. I would go with Pilar to buy ingredients and take a bag full of products to home economics class, where Mrs. Valentín preached over and over the importance of a balanced diet for the family. Out of sheer boredom I would look out the window at what was happening in the corridors until That One came and gave me a meaningful look, and when I left I would meet him you-know-where and we would fool around for as long as we wanted.

Pilar read labels scientifically: products to clean the toilets, bathtub, glass and mirrors, silver and bronze; wax for the floors and wooden furniture. She knew all the kinds of mops, brooms, and dust brushes, and the varieties of chamois and rags. She went to all the Tupperware demonstrations and bought the whole collection. The house's shelves and closets were bursting, since several times a week she would go shopping at the capital's best boutiques. She acquired the latest fashions and styles, while I engaged in kisses and squeezes with the Other in the backyard, the kitchen, and the living room and hid from That One so that he didn't have a fit of jealousy. You could say I was a precocious girl. Precocious, the girl was.

Pilar could be seen walking through the market square between stands selling vegetables and plantains, cilantro and gourds, kitchen implements and washtubs, with her latest lime-green linen suit and her pearl necklace from Mallorca that she had bought in a jewelry store in the capital. She was seen going into the botáni-cas, where the Rose of Jericho slept the sleep of the forgotten in rice sacks, little jet hands swung from gold chains, and the smell and colors of the spices invited one to make love in the swim-ming pool under the light of the moon. The vendors watched this woman approach their stands with her long black tresses and her round body like a ripe grapefruit, and forgot the misfortunes of their lives.

Every other week, Pilar had an appointment with the hair-stylist and the manicurist, and once a month she visited the seamstress with a friend. Pilar would take me in the old Plymouth to spend the afternoon with her friend's daughters. Pilar's friend would climb into the Plymouth and I would climb into bed with my amiguitas. [Este era un gato] We would throw a blanket over ourselves, take our clothes off, and experiment with all kinds of pointed implements. We practiced kisses, squeezes, and fights like the angry lovers in the movies we saw. Other times we would open the lady of the house's drawers and closets, and dress up as cabaret dancers. [Este era un gato] Feathers, shawls, wraps, pearl and rhinestone necklaces, corsets, push-up bras, [que tenía los pies de trapo] spike-heeled shoes, silk panties, and stockings that we made fit with safety pins. We walked through the house dressed like [y la cabecita al revés] a carnival of whores. Exhausted, we would take a bath and walk naked into the kitchen to eat corn cakes and drink glasses of Coca-Cola, until Pilar came to pick me up and her friend yelled, "What are you girls doing naked in the kitchen?"

Pilar made sure that her time was not wasted, keeping up the appearance of a happy married woman living in a modern housing development, with an apron and high-heeled shoes, but her nerves betrayed her. Her loneliness and lack of contact with her husband confused her. She cried over the corners of those shining walls, and on the few occasions when she slept, she awoke anxious or in a bad mood. Sometimes she dreamed of Bella reciting poetry on an arid mountain devoid of vegetation, or she dreamed of the power of a harem sultana, her hands covered with the jewels of the dynasty and her skin perfumed with exotic fragrances. They would mint gold coins in her honor, and on Friday afternoons her name would be proclaimed from the pulpit of the mosque. Furthermore, her power as a sultana would allow her to choose several warriors with strong chests and tight butts, who would hold her and stroke her bones to ecstasy.

"I feel useless and empty; I have the feeling that something's going on out there and I'm missing it," she confessed to her doctor. "Mijita, what are you saying? You're doing everything right, tending to your husband, your family, being available and in a good mood, keeping your house clean, all the things that are important for the family's well-being, what you need is to have a few more kids, having just one is against nature, mija, are you going to church? I'll give you a prescription for barbiturates for when you feel nervous."

"Squeeze out more kids? Never!"

And how did Pilar protect herself from becoming pregnant? Well, the same way everyone else did: from nightshade tea to keeping her legs closed so the member couldn't get in. Sometimes she thought she should get her tubes tied. Half the country was doing it, but she said to herself, "No way! Let the men get cut, I'm not cutting my tubes. Go tell it somewhere else, or like La Negra Tomasa said, porque yo también soy guapa, don't even tell me about it, especially knowing that my husband would take a broom in a wig to bed."

My kind readers will not be surprised to hear that Pilar left the doctor's office como agua pa' chocolate and went straight to Abuelo Cristóbal's house. There he was. Abuelo Cristóbal, prostrate in his cot with an attack of dengue fever. Pilar put a hand on his forehead and covered the old man up as best she could. She took the mosquito netting and tucked it under the mattress. She left the room to find the servant girl and couldn't find her anywhere. Outside, the roosters' incessant crowing was reaching desperate levels and she decided to go down to the patio to see what was going on. The roosters, desperate with hunger and thirst, were crowing madly. She found the sack of corn and began to scatter it through the holes in the wire. She calmly poured water into every trough she could see and swept the yard clear of leaves and garbage.

An unusual sound like a woman's groan made her walk toward the house, and when she entered the henhouse, she found the servant girl impaled on the milkman's spike. She was groaning as if something ached her; but her face was submerged in the deepest of pleasures. Pilar was left frozen to the spot. When the milkman realized that Pilar was an audience to the scene, he tossed the girl off him. The girl ran out to the yard. The milkman tried to put his pants on, but he was so confused that he couldn't, and was left with his balls in the air. He jumped over the fence buck-naked.

Pilar went up to the house and from the window observed the servant girl hiding behind a tree; she also observed each rooster in its cage. Each and every one was an aggressive male with sharp feet and claws. At the end of each back toe there was a sharp claw. The crest stood up like a fiery axe; his spur shone with its own light. She could distinguish clearly the silhouette of the head, torso, the long neck, the feet with the spur in the middle.

14

[Take a lock of the man's beard, cut as close to his ear as possible, and find a silver coin that he's been carrying around for at least half a day. Put both things on to boil in a new gray dish filled with wine. This is the perfect recipe to make a man love you.] Posing in bathing suits with wet bodies, the tourists take pictures of each other. The children throw themselves into the water, play with the sand, and look for shells. The adults sunbathe or go down to the water to splash themselves. A little army of brightly-colored kites disappears among the palm, almond, and tamarind trees. The tails that dance in the breeze are infected with knives. If you don't watch your kite, it will be cut and irreparably wounded.

"Do you want some tamarind? Come on, I'll show you how to open them. You put them on the sand, and with this sharp rock you pound them *smash*!!! until the rind gives way and then a sticky pulp comes out. Then you suck it. Come on, try it."

"Minerva, how could you think of giving such a bitter fruit to that child!" Claudia Luz exclaimed.

"What are you worrying for, Carmen? Tamarinds are nutritious, and children need to learn to eat a little bit of everything."

"Minerva's right; you have to feed children a little bit of everything. When I have mine, they'll even eat dirt," Carmen said.

"They'll have to, because with what that soldier boyfriend of yours earns, I don't think you'll have enough of anything else in that house," Minerva answered.

"¡Cómo eres, Minerva! You don't care anything about motherhood. How many children do you want to have, Carmen?" Cecilia asked.

"I will give birth over and over and over until I pop, but not here. I'm going to marry my soldier and leave the country. Outside this country, things will go better for us."

"But, muchacha, such a hurry to be out of here."

"And why not? Everyone's doing it. It's the most natural thing, the easiest way to get out of that poor neighborhood. I'm fed up with problems. How is it my fault that I'm very pretty and didn't get involved with those nationalists, all crazy and starving, fighting for la patria? What patria? What do I care about the problems of la patria? Unless it's la patria of my bed, my house, a late-model Ford on the street waiting for me. . . . So last night in doña Matilde's bar, they went in and arrested This One, That One, and the Other? Because they're vagos. What do I care, let them take them all, I'll help them keep finding people."

"I think I'll do the same thing. I'll finish college here and go to Madrid to study medicine. I'll live in student lodgings. I have it all planned out," affirmed Cecilia.

"And Mami and Papi know about your plans . . . ?"

"No . . . but they suspect something. They ask me tons of questions and I avoid them, make like I don't understand, because if they find out about my plans, they'll get all their spirits after me."

Claudia Luz listened to Cecilia talk about her plans while Minerva played on the swings in the park. Carmen was lying on the grass, watching two wounded kites as they plunged to the earth at a frightening speed.

"Let's go, it's getting dark. There's a spiritist session today, and you know they want us home early," said Claudia Luz.

"I'm really sick of these spiritist sessions."

"Yeah, ditto."

"Oh, stop complaining."

Arms linked, surrounded by the cacophony of children and ice-cream-and-chewing-gum sellers, the women headed for the Escambrón Hotel, passed a group of tourists with cameras and brightly colored shirts, and headed toward Avenida Ponce de León. The warm afternoon slowly became a hot night with a dry breeze off the water. The sound of the dry leaves mixed with the scream of a red-tailed hawk searching for a mate.

The session at my grandparents' house began at the same time as always. RMC asked for permission to enter the mesa blanca, Abuelo welcomed him, and RMC moved into the body of one of the mediums. "Do the people of Puerto Rico have a hygienic life? How many Puerto Ricans brush their teeth before going to bed? How many take care of their sight? How many delouse themselves? We might even be the most careless people in that respect. Public hygiene, hygiene in cities and in the country, has not gotten very much attention from those who are supposed to be in charge of it." [YOU HEAR THAT, VIEJA?]

The medium fixed her hair, asked for a glass of cold water since (she said) she had been on a long trip, and dried the sweat off her forehead. The women fanned their faces and the men dried their sweat with handkerchiefs, but not Minerva. She had been looking under the table for some time. She had the feeling that something was moving, but couldn't put her finger on what. It was the medium's skirt. She glanced around, and no one else's petticoats were moving. The medium was barking out the words that RMC put in her brain and her skirt floated in what seemed to be a private whirlwind. Minerva got up from her chair and went to stand next to the medium.

"In a well-managed country, where life is really civilized, you wouldn't even *think* of having a populace filled with ringworms and parasites. Unfortunately, that's what has happened on this island. Although if we analyze the whole thing, we'll see that it's a condition of the tropics: what we live here on this island when the sun turns our reason to toffee. That's why I agree with what the governor of the island has said recently." RMC was continuing his speech.

"Your novena is over!" the medium shouted suddenly. "Your novena is over, you can leave now! I'm going to light a candle to La Candelaria for you so you'll go peeeeeeeacefully, but around here, never come baaaaaack."

There wasn't even the slightest doubt, an evil being had taken over the temple. It must have been a witch.

"Alejo que el mal alejas, aleja a los malos ratos . . . y aleja a los insensatos que lleguen aquí," demanded Abuela María while she knocked on wood and reached for the jar with the Rose of Jericho. "Alejo que el mal alejas, aleja a los malos ratos . . ."

The medium began to sing and dance; she shouted curses, lifted her skirt, and sat on Abuelo Juan's lap. With one hand she touched his dick and with the other she picked her nose. Everyone else was in the back room watching TV, and a second later she was back there. Fernando almost wet himself; Claudia Luz started, fell off the bed, and landed next to Cecilia; Carmen didn't even notice because she was taking a bath; Minerva, the grandparents, and the parishioners chased the medium into the room and, after much effort, removed her. Five parishioners together lifted her by her arms, after she had popped open the zipper of her suit, unhooked her bra, and lowered her panties, leaving herself buck-naked. Everything happened very fast, and at the instant that the grandparents entered the room, the medium was already caressing Fernando's body. The poor boy, wide-eyed, was trying to do the impossible and get that being off him.

"Alejo que el mal alejas, aleja a los malos y viciosos, all those who let themselves be influenced by the Man with the Cloven

Hoof," Abuela María repeated. The medium finally fell uncon-
scious, sweating. She woke up, got dressed, and says she never
found out what happened that night.

"What do you mean she never found out? Liar! Caressing Fernando's body with her old wickedness," Minerva replied to Pilar
when the latter asked, "What happened last night at the temple?"

"I just told you. One of the ladies that frequent the temple
got it on with my brother last night. That was the extraordinary
thing, besides RMC's diatribe. Last night he started talking about
hygiene. I think the witches sent a spirit to play a trick on us
and get RMC to shut his mouth. If you could have seen Papi and
Mami's faces! You would have died laughing."

"I can imagine. I think it's time for RMC to retire."

I jumped into the conversation without being invited and
said, "But Mami, hygiene is very important. Once a month the
health nurse comes to my school and repeats her speech about
how hygiene helps to eliminate parasites, fungus, viruses, green
lice, typhus, and bedbugs, so that we can control the tubercu-
losis that's messing up people's lungs and that's why you see
them walking around with their bodies all hunched over. And
there's more; the health nurse never gets tired of saying that
hygiene makes the organism stronger, but in order for that to
happen, you have to bathe every day. In elementary school, the
health nurse shaved a lot of kids' heads and gave out bags of
camphor to put in the drawers at home, and in high school she
gave out new combs and brushes and taught the kids how to
use D-E-O-D-O-R-A-N-T."

"That girl sounds like she works for the government!" Minerva
yelled.

"I told you so, but none of you believed me."

That night while Pilar listened to the news on Canal Dos,
the governor appeared live to give a short but important message on hygiene. "A campaign has been started against filth and
parasites. Sanitation authorities are in charge of this project,

which we anticipate will be a complete success, given that we can rely on the help of the health department. Our goal is to make this island's citizens a model of cleanliness; therefore, I have instructed the Insular Police to close the brothels and call houses as a way to control venereal disease. This includes the old homes of the famous Concha la Tetona, Siete Varas la Gallega, Lula la Ojos, and Madame Chloë the Haitian." [IS NOTHING SACRED?!]

Tía Claudia Luz announced her marriage to the Gringo on a clear December morning, and since she didn't care about religious ceremonies, she stated, "I'm getting married by a judge in three days."

"What do you mean you're getting married and how come you haven't said anything?" Carmen exclaimed.

"The marriage ceremony is not transcendent, not important; what *is* is the commitment to the other person and that's something transcendent, very intimate, very personal."

"Birds of a feather. Congrats, sis," Minerva said to her, while Cecilia gave her sister a big hug. The grandparents didn't say a word, probably because of the shock the news caused. A few days later, when they had recovered, the grandparents began preparations for the wedding reception. To which Claudia Luz responded, "Don't worry, I'm not interested in parties, either."

"Sounds great to me," Fernando said. "That way you don't have to throw money out the window."

"Count on us," Pilar said. "I think it's wonderful that you're starting a family."

The marriage was performed in a courtroom in San Juan, and from there the couple moved to the experimental farm in Guaynabo where the University of Puerto Rico grew avocados and citrus fruit. The Gringo worked as a botanist and surveyor there. They would live in one of the little wooden houses that the farm made available to its married employees. Tía Claudia Luz would devote herself to seeing to her husband, having many children, and waiting for him every evening seated on the balcony of their house.

When the first child was born, the Gringo didn't feel altogether well. He coughed at night, and the phlegm, which had originally been clear, was now thick and red. Nonetheless, they had a big party at the farm to celebrate their son's birth. The Gringo arranged for the peasants who worked the farm to roast a suckling pig. The celebration began on a Saturday morning, with the whole family gathered together. The grandparents saw the baby for the first time and Abuelo Juan said, "This boy needs greater protection. He's a restless, lonely spirit that has been wandering through space for many generations. And your husband doesn't look too good, either."

Abuela Minerva went into the baby's room with Tía Claudia Luz and invoked Eusapia Palladino: "Things aren't going well and there's no cause to celebrate. That boy is surrounded by bad company. He came to this world like a knife to cut the heads off the dead. That is a soul filled with sorrow. You need to baptize him with mineral water from the baths at Coamo; you need to pray over him the prayer for unfortunate spirits. And his father you should cover with Congo incense, Baño San Miguel, ground garlic, papaya, and rue to attract happiness and good fortune," said Eusapia Palladino.

"And the Rose of Jericho?"

"It's no good in these cases."

Back then, if they diagnosed you with perforated lungs, they recommended that you go to the country to breathe pure air. The air, rest, and good food would mend your lungs by magic little by little. That was the prescription the doctor gave to the Gringo. The latter asked for a transfer to an experimental farm in the mountains of Arecibo, sure that the Atlantic air that blew over that coast would improve his health, while Claudia Luz took care of her baby and moved back to the grandparents' house. Everyone knew that the Gringo had the unmentionable disease, the one that stops your breathing and makes a red fluid come from your nose and mouth.

Claudia Luz decided to take an active part in the situation. She enrolled in nursing school, and overnight she became an expert in antibiotics and anesthetics, bacteria, germs, viruses, cells, glands, and blood cells. It was Tía Claudia Luz's goal to see to her husband's health personally, and as if that weren't enough, she asked around in the family but of no one in particular, "Does anyone in this family know the old women of the Caño?"

"I do," replied Pilar.

One Saturday afternoon Pilar and Tía Claudia Luz went down to the labyrinth of alleyways, mangrove roots, and puddles of water, shit, and urine. The old women were helping a customer right then, and they had to wait. While they waited, the neighborhood children approached, and Pilar took seven coins and tossed them into the air, and those lice-infested, smelly children got into a fight over seven cents. While they waited, cries and screams were heard. A high-pitched shout was followed by soft groaning and crying. One of the old women said, "Don't make so much noise, girl, someone might come."

Pilar and Claudia Luz approached the shack. In a dirty, smelly cot was a girl covered in blood. The old women's hands were coated and there was a black clot three inches across, thrown on the ground like a piece of salted meat. The girl was crying and moaning from the pain. Claudia Luz asked, "Can we help?"

Tía Claudia Luz immediately began to clean the girl. Pilar went to get water, and they bathed the girl from head to toe. The old woman made a tea full of malt and anamú, which is good for stopping hemorrhages, and the girl drank the tea until she fell asleep. Pilar and Claudia Luz got under a stream of water from a public spigot and washed their faces, hands, and feet. While the girl slept, the old women stood near the stream of water and Claudia Luz recounted her husband's misfortune.

"That's not all. A lot more is going to happen to your husband, because that body's health is stagnating in the veins; there's a sword across his soul and his spirit is condemned to human vice. It wouldn't hurt to make an infusion of rue and mint and splash it all over his body. No, it wouldn't hurt," recommended one of the old women, as she pulled a thin snake out of a barrel. She broke the animal's neck with her hands and a spurt of black blood covered her fingers. She wrapped the snake's body in an old newspaper and gave Tía Claudia Luz instructions on how to make a soup out of the animal. [Cruz divina llena de luz, drive out the demon.]

16

The move to Arecibo, the doctor's prescriptions, and Tía Claudia Luz's care helped to improve the Gringo's health. Little by little, his face took on a more human color and his hair began to shine again. Soon he began to take short walks around the neighborhood, becoming interested in what was happening in the neighborhood, especially the community education program that the mayor had started in that area. After consulting with his bosses, he agreed to participate in this program by taking a few boys as apprentices. El Gringo then prepared a program of classes on the practice of grafting, devoting his mornings to this agricultural practice. El Gringo was passionate about everything having to do with the study of soil, but what he desired most was to take apprentices and teach them what he knew about it.

The mayor and the Gringo became great friends, and once in a while and from time to time, the mayor would stop by the farm to evaluate the progress of the apprentices in the science of grafting, since they were the future of this area. Furthermore, every time the aforementioned mayor saw a lice-infested street kid, he would send him to the Gringo's house, where the boy would get a good bath and a change of clothes, and from there be sent to the farm to learn about grafting: splice grafts, approach grafts, grafts when the scion is open like a wound, like an exposed anus, both plants alive, in perfect condition to develop in such a way that they will constitute an organism capable of growing and producing fruit. The Gringo with his two dogs—he had two lame mutts who were always getting in the way, sticking their noses where they didn't belong, barking at any horned toad that they found in the grass, always a nuisance, always ill-timed.

The Gringo had by now completely recovered his health. He felt strong and was fully enjoying his retreat. This was confirmed by Danilo Sepúlveda, one of the peasants who worked on the farm:

> "It seems like working in the field allowed him a certain amount of tranquility, but what he most wanted to do was be able to share things with his apprentices. Sometimes with all of them at once, or privately one-on-one. Thus he instructed them in the art of grafting. The kind that involves applying a pointed piece of skin in the orifice of the stock. The one that involves sticking a splice of the new plant between the bark of the stock, the one that happens when you put it under the bark of the stock with a decisive cut, a piece of bark, then later it comes out through the cut like a kind of bud." [Tape 2. Side A.]

The variety of citrus fruits that he was able to obtain with the help of his apprentices, as well as the beauty of his avocados, made him popular in that region. Agriculturists from all over the island came to his house in search of a way to improve their harvests. The Gringo's advice was always followed with astounding success, but at sundown he would gather with his apprentices to improve their secret games, completely forgetting his condition, the doctor's recommendations, what his wife and family would say, erasing his son from his memory, contenting himself with the moment of ecstasy and total abandon.

> "He paid me good money not to leave the farm when he had work and I, curious but not a gossip, would spy on him through the keyhole and between the shrubs of the greenhouse. I hid between the branches, which were dry, bare, and bound like the wounds on a traffic accident victim. I hid with the lame mutts who sniffed the inside of shit-filled shorts." [Tape 2. Side B.]

PLANT GRAFTING

A caterpillar infestation has appeared, infecting recent grafts on farms in Arecibo and other towns. In accordance with the indications of the entomologist from the Agricultural Experimental Station at the University of Puerto Rico, the recent grafts are being strongly attacked by both large and small caterpillars of two different species. These insects rapidly devour the leaves of the grafts and sometimes also eat the lianas. When they have devoured all the foliage, they move in great swarms to other shoots. If not counteracted in time, the infestation can cause serious damage to the grafts and other valuable crops. According to the entomologist, in December of 1918 there was a similar attack in the northwestern part of the island, from Arecibo to Aguadilla. Scientists have found that dusting with insecticides, alone or in combination, has given good results. The combination of one percent parathion and five percent DDT or DDD is, apparently, the ideal way to combat the aforementioned infestations. *[Finca y Hogar: The Magazine for Farm and Family]*

[I wanted to see you, and not to see you.] The Gringo's death was sudden. It was to be expected. Physical exercise was not exactly what the doctor ordered. Before he died, he specified in his will that his remains should be cremated and the ashes scattered in the Atlantic Ocean. Death is the worst thing that can happen in these cases. It reveals enormous secrets.

The whole family wore black—on an ordinary day at eleven o'clock on a radiant morning. The whole family met in the plaza in Arecibo. Claudia Luz carried the Gringo's ashes in a metal box. We walked to the open sea. The waves beat against the stones with the ferocity of a starving enemy. A group of Claudia Luz's classmates waited on the shore. One of them approached Claudia Luz and gave her a little envelope. Abuelo Juan and Abuela María tried to say a few words before scattering the ashes in the sea, but the sea was in a fierce mood that day and a sudden wave forced them to run back toward the highway. Cecilia, Pilar, and Carmen helped Claudia Luz get back on her feet; Minerva and Fernando began walking to the square while Felipe took me by the hand. I could smell the cologne on his wrist. I took my father's warm hand and let myself be led. That day Pilar was stunning in a tight black linen suit and a necklace of freshwater pearls that she had gotten at a jeweler's in San Juan.

After the ceremony, Claudia Luz decided to stay at the house on the farm in Arecibo in order to pack up the Gringo's belongings. Pilar and I stayed to keep her company. The family left for San Juan that afternoon with the little boy. After we stopped at a grocer's to get what we needed for dinner, we went to the Gringo's house. Claudia Luz went to the kitchen, got herself a glass of water, and went into the deceased's room. She pulled the envelope out of her purse, opened it and took out a barbiturate, which she put in her mouth. She lay down on the deceased's bed, still fully dressed, and fell asleep. The next day, somewhat recovered, Tía Claudia Luz got up and went to take a bath. She got undressed and opened the medicine cabinet. Claudia Luz called Pilar and asked, "What's that?" pointing to the open medicine cabinet.

"A plastic dildo."

Curious, Claudia Luz inspected that piece of craftsmanship and set it carefully back in its place. She opened the linen closet and took one of the towels. She got into the tub and noticed a few small drops of blood on the ceramic of the walls. She got out of the bath, opened her suitcase, took out a change of clothes, and without having any coffee, began to dust the furniture and change the sheets. Pilar and I remained in the kitchen. Pilar fixed lunch and I read a *Bohemia* I had found in the living room. Claudia Luz continued cleaning. She went into the Gringo's bedroom, took the sheets off the bed, took the dirty clothes out of the hamper, and began to sweep, but not without first lifting the mattress off the bed. At that instant a pile of photos flew into the air and scattered across the floor. Claudia Luz, half-curious, half-surprised, picked them up. She sat down on the bed and carefully began to flip through them.

[What a catastrophe!] Naked apprentices; [I wanted] apprentices photographed in a nearby shack the way God brought them into the world, taking the risk that a nearby rooster or hen might peck at their horn; apprentices playing together, touching each other's skin and every bit of [to see you] muscle. The widow, horrified, threw the photographs aside, continued rummaging through the room, and found silver spoons; [and not to see you] bottles with narrow ends; smooth, rounded pieces of wood; strings of plastic beads; metal [I wanted to speak to you] handcuffs and kid-leather whips. Poor widow, I can see her, heartbroken, throwing drawers on the ground, breaking mirrors, [and not to speak to you], burning the photos.

Night fell and Tía Claudia Luz continued throwing, burning, and destroying that house piece by piece. Pilar came [I wanted to find you] into the deceased's room, opened [alone] Claudia Luz's purse, and [and I didn't want] pulled out the envelope. She opened it [to find you] and pulled out a barbiturate, got a glass of water and gave it to her.

"Take this."

I wanted to speak to you and not to speak to you; I wanted to
find you and not to find you. I definitely did not want to find
you, either alone or with someone else.] Years later, now recovered,
Tía Claudia Luz used the deceased's pension to buy a house in
a small development quite near the grandparents' house. By that
time, she had finished her nursing studies and was working at
Hospital Pavía. Around then she joined the Oz Project.

"What's that, mija?"

"It's a project that investigates spaceships, Mother. They use big
telescopes to observe the infinite, to see if there's life out there."

"And what do you think?"

"Pilar, why are you asking her? She's obviously stark raving
mad!" Carmen exclaimed.

"I think so; I think there is life, and furthermore, I tend to think
that spirits, souls, and angels are nothing more than interplanetary
beings that want to communicate with us. All I need is proof."

"A bad thing. A bad thing," said Abuelo Juan.

"Why is it a bad thing?" Minerva asked.

"Because you don't need any more proof than what you see every day in this house when the temple is open and when it's not open as well, since the spirits are always welcome here," Abuelo Juan answered.

"Papi, let her do whatever she wants; she's suffered enough to earn it."

"Well, so that you'll keep being so upset, Papi, I suspect that witches are intermediaries on Earth and that they have the powers necessary to communicate with higher beings in other galaxies," Claudia Luz answered.

On the nights when Claudia Luz was not on call at the hospital, she would be on top of some mountain in front of a telescope. Sometimes Pilar and I would go with her. The usual route was this: take the old Plymouth up Highway 1 to the intersection with El Yunque. Turn right and zigzag up the mountain.
Bordering the river.
The rocks.
The little cabins on both sides of the mountains.
The dwarf ferns.
The hovel where an old woman fries bacalaítos.
Yagrumo trees, plantains.
Two little girls on the mountain gathering coffee.
The sign that said "Property of the U.S.A."
The sea on the horizon.
An Englishman. A 250-foot telescope of the Jodrell Bank Observatory in Manchester, property of an Englishman who lived on the island, looked out into the infinite. Out of the corner of his eye, the Englishman watched Tía Claudia Luz as she figured out signs beyond the solar system and the sounds of unknown galaxies. The Englishman would invite me to look through the telescope. I could see pieces of sky and thousands of stars, the

moon in a corner. If I moved the telescope forty degrees I could see the Englishman holding hands with Tía Claudia Luz. If I turned the telescope sixty degrees, I could see Pilar sitting on a rock, her eyes sad as she looked at the immensity of the horizon and the mist covering the vegetation. We spent hours there, trying to reach some invisible, remote, unknown planet that would serve as a source of support and hope. I especially remember my mother staring at the horizon. One night we found the constellation Cetus, 11,000 light years from Earth, and the Englishman and Claudia Luz embraced.

> Was the universe created? Or is it instead eternal like God? There is no doubt that it could not have been made all by itself, and if it were eternal like God, it would not be God's work. Reason tells us that the universe could not have made itself, and not being a work of chance, it must be that of God. How did God create the universe? To coin a phrase: by sheer force of will. Reason tells us that worlds have been formed by the condensation of material scattered in space. Comets are a beginning of a world, still chaotic. The beginning of a being occurs in the chaos of the galaxies. Organic beginnings controlled by an aura—that is, the spirits—gathered together as soon as the force keeping them apart ended, and formed the seeds of all living beings. Where were the organic elements before the earth was formed? That they were in a state of flux, so to speak, in space, in the middle of the spirits or on other planets, waiting for the earth to be created so they could start a new existence on a new globe. Are all the planets inhabited? Yes. And Earthman is far from being (as he thinks he is) the first in intelligence, goodness, and perfection. There are, nonetheless, very vain men who imagine that this little globe has the exclusive privilege of having rational beings. They figure that God created the universe just for them.*

* Rosendo Matienzo Cintrón. *Complete Works* (San Juan: ICP, 1950). I can't remember the page, but you can search for it or ask a librarian; they're that kind of people.

18

On her few free nights, Tía Claudia Luz sat on the balcony of her house until the cloud of sleep descended or the mosquitoes got rid of her. She was really waiting for the Englishman, since in recent times they had become very close. Very late one night, the neighborhood began to go to sleep and she continued dozing in her chair. One of the neighbors says that she looked out the window and saw Claudia Luz accompanied by a gentleman:

> "It seemed curious to me that she would be receiving visits at that hour of the night. So I decided to watch more closely. I realized they were smiling, and felt relieved to think that he was someone she knew.
>
> "A fierce rain poured down on all of us that night; they were hard, fast drops. At sunrise I got up like I always did and opened the windows. The body was there lying on the sidewalk, completely soaked. The neighbors were already beginning to sniff around the scene. Someone called the police, and the rest is common knowledge.

"I knew about the son; it's just that he didn't live with her. He was just a kid who had moved out on his own very young, but that didn't stop him from seeing his mother often. He was very attentive to her. He tended her garden and did all the repairs on the house. He took her to her doctor's appointments, and on the Day of the Dead he took her to the cemetery."

Pilar, trying to understand why one of her nephews had passed away, was reading out loud the witness statement that had appeared in the newspaper that day.

"I never knew my sister had a lover; at her age it seems rather foolish," Felipe said.

"The foolish ones are you men for thinking that we don't itch the same way."

The witness's statement continued:

"The son had been against that relationship, which he considered ridiculous. That night the son got liquored up and decided to drop in on his mother. I heard noises in the yard and decided to look out the window again. I saw the son open the balcony door."*

The son entered the house and found the couple curled up together like two turtledoves. The Englishman woke up, startled, tried to flee, and the struggle began. The Englishman took something heavy off the dresser and hit the other man hard over the head. He didn't think he had killed the boy, just that he had knocked him out. In that fierce rain, he dragged him down to the sidewalk. The water would take care of washing away the blood that was coming from his head. The rain kept flowing while that boy stayed lying in the middle of the sidewalk. The Englishman? They're still looking for him.

The day of my cousin's burial, the great-aunts came to the island, agitated and somewhat confused. As soon as they appeared in the baggage pickup area of the airport, they embraced Abuelo

* These statements can be found in the newspaper *El Imparcial*, March 1955, p. 10.

Juan, and the three of them clung together like three barnacles on the hull of a boat. When they got to the grandparents' house, they took from their purse a little bit of pure cannabis from Jamaica (where the plant grows in silence) and went into the kitchen to boil water. The great-aunts wept and moaned, and their tears fell into that pot of water, turning the liquid into a salty soup into which they sprinkled the cannabis little by little. Between sobs, they passed out cups of that tea to the members of the family. Lethargy overcame every member of my family, including my parents; and one by one, all of us began to find that diurnal somnolence, the kind that makes you feel like you're sleeping with your eyes open, and you can almost hear the "la la la" of a lullaby.

The day of my cousin's burial, the members of the Oz Project held a ceremony in which they invoked the dark firmament saturated with a chaos of stars, dust, crushed ice, unknown metals, and silver-colored earth. They invoked Queen Oz in a far-off, difficult-to-find land populated with exotic, strange beings, and there was no spirit or tormented soul that crossed their path. Yet more proof of the origin of the spirits.

That night we all had mixed-up dreams and Claudia Luz dreamed of a carriage in the firmament pulled by silver horses. The carriage held a gold coffin with her son sleeping in it. If you looked closely, you could see that the corpse's eyelashes and eyebrows were covered with gold nuggets. Eusapia Palladino awoke Claudia Luz with a shout. "Niña, it's me. I'm the one who's taking your son, restless and lonely, to live the infinite dream."

Now Pilar prays for Tía Claudia Luz, now without a husband, lover, or son. Pilar imagines the son's spirit, brusque and excited, moving around the house, asking after Claudia Luz and Pilar both, for his infinite desire to be able to possess another body, another man. She who does not have lovers waiting for her on the balcony. She who would give what she doesn't have to listen to Tía Claudia Luz's story of having him at night in bed with an invented fear, but fortunate: to be almost free.

19

In a family with so many women, marriages were the order of the day. It was the time when at Central High School they still taught Latin "non," a repeated negation of a thing, non, non, non. The country was going one way, and we were going another. Misery loves company. During that same era, Carmen announced her engagement to the little lead soldier. Abuelo Juan gave his blessing to the marriage, but just in case, he went to consult with the Haitians of the Caño.

It had been many years since Abuelo Juan had gone into that territory. Although Fabián was no longer in this world, it seemed prudent to have this consultation even though that was going against the spirits. He had seen too much in this world already, and it's wise to give up Puritanism and consult people who knew much more than he about transparent evil.

"There's nothing wrong or strange about going to have this consultation. I've been a well-to-do man and no one is going to come and trick me. The whole neighborhood knows me."

There in the depths of the mangrove swamp, he found the Haitians smoking tobacco and conversing in a language impossible for him to understand. They were in the middle of a bonfire made of wood shavings in order to keep the mosquitoes from getting to them. The old women that night were airing out their bodies, walking up and down the shores of the Caño. Abuelo Juan ignored them because he doesn't get mixed up with witches. By virtue of the spirits, he asked the presences for help. A man covered himself with a red blanket and wild turkey feathers, took a feather duster made of rags and pigeon feathers, and hit Abuelo Juan several times. They gave him a melcocha of rum with turtle meat and onion, and in his left ear they hung a gold hoop. The old women in the distance could see the ceremony, and laughed 'til their sides hurt every time Abuelo jumped with pleasure.

That night Abuelo Juan arrived at his home with a hangover, for which That One had to be found to help him into bed. Abuelo Juan didn't get up for three days, as he was suffering from severe headaches and vomiting. ["Didn't I tell you, Minga?!"]

Yellow was the color of the dress I wore for the wedding of Tía Carmen and Víctor the Soldier. Yellow lace, a yellow belt that tied around my waist at the back, a yellow ribbon holding my curls back, a yellow as delicate as the color of my aunts' skin.

Pilar liked to look at her daughter, a big girl, a small young woman, a girl with little breasts, a young woman with a little-girl face. A little girl, then.

Pilar was in charge of the wedding gown. One of the photographs of the weddings is the one where you see the bride sitting on one of those little benches that are part of the set that includes a vanity table and mirror. The mirror reflects the bride's back, a pitcher of daisies, calla lilies, baby's breath, and to the right Pilar, sober and elegant in a lilac organza dress, is putting the headpiece and veil on the bride's head. Pilar saw to it personally that the veil was one that would leave a train the length of the aisle. She made sure that the bride's bouquet was calla lilies and ribbons that hung down the train of the gown, since she felt those were the most elegant.

Pilar and the bride looking at the camera lens. Pilar with her luminous skin and her resigned eyes. The lens takes in the rest of the women in the family. They are covering their heads with mantillas to prevent demons from filling the temple.

20

Three months after the wedding, Víctor the Soldier left for war on the ship *Big Fighter*. It was January, and the light of the sun descended transparently over the shore of the sea. It was February and the grandparents' house was flooded with gifts for Tía Carmen. She received linen from Panama and tobacco from Guatemala; hand-woven fabric of the Oaxaca Indians and silver accessories designed by artisans in Honduras. The *Big Fighter* stopped at ports in Hawaii and Japan and the house became an Oriental showroom with kimonos, paper lamps, Oriental folding screens, and silk: raw silk, hand-painted silk with designs of dragons in red and green. Tía Carmen became the envy of the neighborhood.

"You see how she walks? She thinks she's all that."

"Shh, quiet; she might hear you."

"Let her hear me; I'm not scared."

After six months of being away, the letters and gifts to Tía Carmen from her husband became scarce. Every afternoon my aunt sat waiting on the balcony like any Cucarachita Martina and asked over and over about correspondence from her husband. Pilar, being accustomed to her husband's absences, decided to devote some time to Tía Carmen. Here we shall reproduce the dialogue between the two. We shall also reproduce the setting.

In those days, radio soap operas were in vogue. I can assure you that the following dialogue could be confused with any modern TV soap opera, but I can also assure you that it is really between my mother and one of my aunts.

The scene takes place in a living room with a rattan sofa and cushions with bright tropical designs. A vase filled with plastic flowers on a dining table, also made of rattan, with a glass top.

PILAR: What's the problem with Víctor's correspondence? (*Says* PILAR *as she curls up on the cushions.*)

CARMEN: I don't know and I'm dying of anxiety. (*The detail of the neckline of* CARMEN's *outfit is one that draws the eye. The character knows it, and she makes that part of her body stand out by sticking her chest out.*)

PILAR: You have to take things calmly. You can't lose your head over these island men. (*Now* PILAR *strokes her eyelashes with her right thumb.*)

CARMEN: But I'm worried about him.

PILAR: This "love" thing is a fantasy or a miracle, and I don't believe in either one anymore. (*PILAR inspects her nails.*)

CARMEN: How can you talk like that?

PILAR: Experience will tell you what to do. For the moment, don't even think that you're a widow, because I believe Víctor will be around for a long time. He's not dumb enough to go die in some stupid war. Be calm and devote yourself to waiting for him.

CARMEN: Do you think I should go see the old women?

PILAR: The old women don't manage wars. War is a men's thing.

CARMEN: Then I'll find a santero. Those people, they don't mess around.

PILAR: They can't help you, either.

CARMEN: I don't know you, Pilar. What's happened to you in all these years?

PILAR: I married your brother.

CARMEN: But you have all kinds of luxuries. You can't complain. You shop at the best stores and your daughter is divine. What are you complaining about?

That night, after the ritual of cosmetics, creams, and cleansing lotions, Pilar took a barbiturate and dreamed of a blind husband buried in the deepest cave of the northern coast. An Aparecido with a transparent body but solid feelings got her out of bed, pushed her toward the black Plymouth parked in the yard, and stroked her feelings without touching her, holding her in the shape of her body's cunt. An Aparecido appeared in Tía Carmen's dreams. An Aparecido with a multicolored face and glittering eyes, dressed in white, offered her advice in the name of Eleguá. You give Eleguá goat, jutía, rooster, chicken, and you also offer him Jamaican slider, make the sign of the cross three times, and sing him the "Prayer to the Seven African Potencies" at the full moon. Tía Carmen approaches and touches his transparent tabard. An Aparecido entered and left the Plymouth and came to my window, monitoring my sleep. As soon as he reached my window, a group of little birds filled the room, waving their arms-which-are-not-arms, and I didn't know if I was crying for the spirits, for the Aparecido, or for Pilar and Felipe, who couldn't attend to my grief.

From that night on, for seventy-four days, Tía Carmen offered goats, roosters, and chickens in sacrifice to Eleguá. Abuelo Cristóbal got her the best prey to deposit next to the candles and statues of saints on an improvised altar in her kitchen. On each full moon she sang him the "Prayer to the Seven African Potencies," which begins, "O Seven Potencies that surround the Saint among Saints! I humbly kneel before you, a miraculous court, to implore you to return my husband. Loving father who protects all creation, animate and inanimate, I ask you in the Most Sacred and Sweet Name of Jesus, to attend to my petition. May you hear me, Changó, Ochún, Yemayá, Obatalá, Ogún, Orula, and especially Eleguá. Bring my husband back to me. Amen."

The miracle came through. One morning the postman brought the longed-for letter. Tía Carmen fearfully gave the letter to Pilar, who read each sentence, each word slowly as she fanned herself with her fan with black ribs. That night Pilar dreamed of the war and its mountains of skeletons scattered across the middle of the countryside; she dreamed of Víctor rubbing his body against Tía Carmen's, and from that day on she understood how complex the secret of infidelity is. A secret which, like any good secret, remains hidden beneath itself.

Dear Carmen,

    I was wounded by a bullet. Suddenly I felt strange. It seemed like your face was very close to mine. I felt myself pass out, and I remember that a comrade unbuckled my belt. I suppose I must have been unconscious for a moment. I think I remained there for several hours, because when I woke up the stars were shining in the sky. There was a strange quietness all around me and your face was nearby. I stretched out my hand and touched my comrade; I called him and he didn't answer. I fell back, exhausted. Later I found out what had happened. The fighting had ceased and I was left among the dead with my comrades who had fallen, never to rise again. The fear of death invaded me. I don't remember anything else. When I woke up, I was in the hospital, where they have treated me very well. I write to you from the bottom of my heart.

    I think about you night and day. Your smell excites me, and despite my desolation, I need to feel your body against mine. In the middle of this hospital, I imagine you in front of me, naked.

                                 Forever yours,
                                 Víctor

21

After the war, the few men left alive returned to the island. Víctor returned on a chilly Christmas Day, and the family threw a big party to welcome him home. The kitchen was full of pots bubbling and plates of arroz con gandules, pigs' feet, gandinga, carey encebollao, crab stew, and boiled lobster. Abuelo Cristóbal brought the season's best rum, and Abuela María made pineapple wine and pitorro rum. Tía Minerva tossed colored paper streamers into the air and lit sparklers, which twinkled with light. The house was full of guests; Cecilia and Felipe passed plates of food and Felipe served drinks. Víctor could be seen talking to Pilar: they could be seen together in the bathroom doorway, on their way to the backyard, and under the mahogany tree.

That night Pilar sat down at her vanity and picked up her hairbrush. Slowly she brushed each lock of hair from top to bottom. She brushed carefully until the sounds of the brush against her skull became the only sound in the room. Pilar had by now become one more woman who spied on men and kept them under surveillance as frantically as a crazed rival, but as covertly as the way the government spied on the island's inhabitants.

A few days later she was seen with Víctor at a motel facing the sea on the road to Loíza. A room full of windows, an uncomfortable bed with a second-hand mattress and cheap cotton sheets, a bathroom without tiles and a floor of unadorned concrete. Pilar cared little for these details, throwing herself at that man as she never had done with Felipe. They struggled passionately until they were left sweaty and glowing with happiness. That day, the music of the waves, the breeze from the sea, and the palette of turquoise of the ocean took root in my mother's heart.

From that day on, the lovers saw each other countless times. They would take the road up to the pastures in the mountains, where they would stop at every motel in the area, then end in some bar full of cigarette smoke, spending hours enjoying the green highland landscape with a cup of coffee or a shot of rum.

Other times they would take the roads along the coast and bathe in the sea where they would engage in carnal gymnastics or stop by a little rustic cabin that belonged to a friend of Víctor's. The property was next to land where there was a coconut grove bordering the sea. It was a summer residence without luxuries, with two mattresses thrown on the floor and a few chairs. The icebox was always empty, and Pilar took it upon herself to fill it with water, beer, and rum, which Víctor's friend appreciated. Pilar and Víctor spent several months cuddled up together in the car, up and down the road, without anyone in the family ever suspecting.

A year later, Víctor the Soldier informed the family that he would be leaving again for Panama, but this time he would take his wife. They would live at Fort Clayton, in the Canal Zone.

"What are you going to do there if you've already finished in the army?" asked Abuelo Juan.

"I'm going to work with the Intelligence Service."

"Sounds great to me," Felipe answered, stroking Pilar's neck. My mother heard the news and stood staring out at the horizon, her gaze stopping on the street sweeper cleaning the gutters. A scrawny cat slept under a tree, and the neighborhood loony dropped his shorts in front of a passerby. She kept staring until she no longer saw the street or its houses, the traffic, or the neighbors. A little voice inside her asked, *Pilar, what do you think you're doing?*

From Pier One of the naval base on Cataño Bay, Tía Carmen and Víctor the Soldier left on the *Big Fighter*. At Guantánamo they had a seven-hour stopover, since the boat needed to load up on technological equipment. The couple decided to disembark and have lunch at the officers' club. There they gorged themselves on a stew of fresh crab and lobster while they listened to a big band play mambos, qué rico el mambo, mambo qué rico es, es, es. Four days later the coast of the canal could be seen, and less than twelve hours later they were set up in Fort Clayton, a field of wooden houses, filled with jacaranda and cedar trees.

The house was sprawling, filled with hallways and corridors, and the roof was high and arched. The only problem was that they had to share the house with a host of bats, who during the day clung to the arches of the porch roof like black specks, and at night went out to the valley. A mulatto girl cleaned the arches of the porch roof every day with leaves from the cedar tree attached to a long piece of wood, with the hope that the little devils would not return, but as soon as the first shaft of light appeared, a line of bats would head straight to that house.

Besides the mulata, an Indian woman cooked plantains and codfish three times a week, since the rest of the time the couple went to the officers' club, where they enjoyed a dinner-dance. Bands came from Cuba and played their *son*, and Sylvia de Grasse sang Panameña, panameña, panameña vida mía. The couples jumped around without rhyme or rhythm, their bodies moving with the trembling typical of an epileptic fit. One of the officers' wives watched Víctor the Soldier's ass with great attention, but so did the general secretary of the national House of Deputies and the wife of the country's most important baseball pitcher, who was playing in Mexico at the time.

By the end of seven months' time, Víctor came and went from the president's palace with complete confidence. The training in the intelligence school was rigorous; more than half the candidates were eliminated. To top it all off, he had to go through all kinds of evaluations and interrogations, but his audacity was proved time and time again. At the end of a year, Víctor was friends with deputies and government officials and began to travel to the provinces of Boca del Toro, Chiriquí, Coclé, Colón, San Blas, Panamá, Darién, Herrera, Los Santos, and Veraguas. In the bars of Colón he could be seen drinking with members of the National Assembly and high government officials while they informed him about the facilities for exporting crops and machinery. His job was exactly that: to socialize in the highest circles, and Tía Carmen could not get over her astonishment. Every other day she had to get dolled up in her best dresses and attend, with her husband, high society baptisms, parties, and receptions. The couple would return home exhausted. Then Víctor the Soldier had to spend long hours at night and into the early morning at the dining room table with compass and ruler, sketching the parlors he had visited, since drawing up diagrams of government facilities and military property was his job; the balls, birthday parties, and receptions provided his excuse.

Tía Carmen had two children while she learned to cook pickled pigs' feet with gherkins and potatoes harvested from Mt. Barú volcano. When her second son was born, she seized the opportunity to have her fallopian tubes tied, since the method was simple and half the world was doing it. Two children are more than enough, but happiness is not eternal, my dear readers. One May day, Tía Carmen had her first asthma attack, thanks to the bat shit that was wreaking havoc on the roof of the house. The doctor recommended a few days in the military hospital while the military police fumigated the house. The mulatto girl took charge of the children, the Indian woman kept cooking plantains with codfish over an improvised burner, and Tía Carmen's husband kept up his routine of receptions and balls.

One afternoon the mulatto girl and the Indian woman came to the military hospital looking very distressed. The mulatto girl began to speak. "The man of the house, your husband, he's chasing around a gringa piece of tail, or maybe the gringa is following your husband's tail around. I saw them with these very eyes. I was cleaning up the mess that the kids left in the back room, when that lady came to the house, asked for your husband, and sat in the parlor across from his room. That husband of yours, he was in His Grace's room. He opened the door and took off his clothes so the gringa could see him naked. Then that lady smiled."

Tía Carmen cried so much salt water that you could easily have filled one of the sluices of the canal with her tears. When she left the sanatorium, she paid those good women very well for their services. One morning when Tía Carmen's husband left for a trip to the provinces, she left the children with the mulatto girl and went out to the home of the commander of the fort. In the solitude of his office, Tía Carmen said to him, "My husband is sleeping with your wife. And so I've come so you will help me straighten them out. I don't want a court-martial; that wouldn't be good for you or for me. As for my husband, I want you to intervene so that they send him to the front lines of the next battle. I will wait for what's left of him at this fort, if he comes back. You'll know best what to do with your wife."

Tía Carmen left the commander's office. The noonday sun burned the road. The jacaranda trees stood upright and stoic, creating a shade where a group of Indians were selling their weavings and clay pots at the base entrance. It was the time of day when the alligators came out of the nearby lake to take their siesta. The blues song that an American soldier was singing woke her from her lethargy: Georgina, tell me when are you going to be mine. Tía Carmen turned around and walked over to where that man was.

22

"Who wants more coffee?" Minerva asked.

"Order another round, because I have an announcement to make," Cecilia said softly.

"Waiter, four cafés con leche!" Minerva called to a round man in his fifties in a red-and-black uniform. "And another cookie for the little girl!"

El Nilo Café was always full of people. The noise of the customers' cups and chairs, the waiters' aluminum trays hitting things, and the continuous hiss of the espresso maker decorated with bronze figures of angels hanging from grapevines—it was one of the preferred meeting places of San Juan's people. At that hour, the sun felt like a thread of gold that strangled the glass panes of the doors, the tables, the floor tiles, and the walls of the establishment. The "little girl" is me, but I am not so little anymore, sitting with my tight capri pants and stylish sweater in between Pilar, Minerva, Claudia Luz, and Cecilia.

"I can guess what you're going to say," Claudia Luz said.

"I have everything ready to go study in Madrid. I have some savings from what I make at the porcelain factory, and I'm expecting to be able to get a scholarship from the government," Cecilia confirmed.

"But you're such an artist with the porcelain already," Minerva said, stroking Cecilia's hair.

"Leave her alone. She wants to go, so she will. Tell us about your job at the factory. Maybe I have a friend who could take over for you when you go to Spain," Claudia Luz said.

"It's a repetitive, monotonous job, but I've learned to handle and mold clay and porcelain, mix paints, clean brushes, light the kiln, let the ceramics cool, and oversee all of it because all the pieces have to be made according to the company's specifications."

"And are you sure you're going there to study and not to look for a husband?" Pilar asked. "I don't think the folks will agree."

"Well, they'll have to agree, because the decision is already made."

"Cecilia, you haven't answered my question."

Cecilia was no longer listening. Amid the noise of the cups and the horns of new and old cars out in the street, Cecilia sat quietly, silent, trying to see as far as she could over the rooftops of the newly constructed high-rises next to the ancient trees. Maybe there she would find the answer.

For two years, Tía Cecilia worked to save every last cent, except the money to go out on Friday nights. She learned to transfer patterns directly to the raw clay, wash the paper of each piece, make original designs for the porcelain, organize the pieces for shipping, and prepare invoices. On Fridays she would go out with her coworkers to a bar owned by an American. The only thing it sold was bottled beer and white rum for fifteen cents a shot. It was a pleasant locale where the morning sun filtered through the fronds of the roof and the smell of saltwater filled the place. That One cleaned tables and washed the glasses and the Other mopped the place every morning. The locale was filled with gringo journalists who argued and debated the day's events with each other.

"Mami, I'm going to Madrid to study medicine," Tía Cecilia informed Abuela María.

"Why don't you study nursing, like your sister Claudia Luz?" Abuelo Juan yelled from his bedroom. "That way you can stay here on the island without going off by yourself to God knows where. I don't want a daughter of mine going out in the world without our protection. It doesn't seem like a good idea."

"You know that my dream is to study medicine, and there are no facilities on this island. And I'll be in Europe. In Spain! Imagine! You can come visit me whenever you want."

"And with what money?"

"I'll figure it out, just like dozens of puertorros every year."

With a daughter as stubborn as the rest, Abuelo Juan, worried by Cecilia's plans, called together the spirits that very night. Returning to the Caño was not even taken into consideration. The drunken experience of that night had left him drained; and all for the best it was, too, since he learned not to defy the spirits. Eusapia Palladino entered the body of a medium that night of intense rain brought on by the hexes of the old women of the Caño. She arrived rather wet, splashing water on the parishioners. A lady sneezed a couple of times, and Abuela María went to the kitchen to get some hand towels so people could dry off.

"There is a soul in torment who is mixing bat crap so that the girl will go off. It's more than one soul, because there's another one that has her crucified with brambles so no man will get attached to her, and another that's throwing soap in her eyes so she can't see what's around her. This seems like witchcraft."

"What can be done?" Abuelo Juan asked in desperation.

"Nothing," Eusapia Palladino answered.

"What do you mean, nothing; what are you all good for?"

Abuelo Juan asked Abuela María for a cup of linden tea. He drank the tea and the next day went straight to Felipe's office.

"Papi, you're worrying too much about Cecilia," Felipe stated.

"I'm worried because the spirits don't look well upon that trip."

"You know that I don't care about what the spirits think. Besides, you need to become modern, explore new possibilities. What's wrong with my sister wanting to go to school away from the island like so many other Puerto Ricans? She needs to get out of this province. Don't worry about the money. I'll take care of it."

Resigned, Abuelo Juan made the decision to support his daughter, who wanted to go study medicine in Spain, but just in case, Pilar and Claudia Luz decided to meddle in the affair. Early one morning, they went to the Caño to talk with the old women. They found them at the mouth of the bridge next to the sea. They had spent the night bathing in the rain because it's good for curing colds. Pilar and Claudia Luz had a lot of faith in those old women and Pilar immediately informed them about Cecilia's plans.

"Demons don't have no tongue or lungs; they don't have teeth or lips, but they can communicate in many ways. To me this looks like the work of the Aparecido. What he's out searching for is a woman who won't give herself to no one and when it's time he can take her. The Aparecido has found his woman and it doesn't matter where she goes, he'll go there too. Give her roosters' balls to eat, mixed with beans. She'll begin to think 'bout what's around here and give up this stuff 'bout goin'. Because thinking 'going, going' she might go; but things ain't right for travelin'."

Pilar and Claudia Luz analyzed the recipe and decided that rooster balls might kill Tía Cecilia by indigestion, and plans for the trip began. Felipe asked Pilar to take charge of everything. Pilar reserved a one-way ticket, New York to Madrid on Trans World Airlines. She packed a suitcase with some winter clothes, which she managed to find in the warehouses on Calle San Francisco. She took the suitcase, got in the Plymouth, and picked me up at school. From there we went to the ranch to see the old women:

"The Aparecido has done it. She's his woman and no one's gonna interfere. He'll take her far away so the spirits of the house can't touch her. The best we can do is give her some kind of amulet."

"That's why I've brought the clothing she's going to take with her. To see if we can put some kind of enchantment on it."

"The best would be an enchantment for the Aparecido. They say he flies at midnight and his guts go in an' out of people who sleep with their mouths open. Then he gets inside women and kisses their darkest parts. The woman feels comfortable and walks with him all over. They say also that when the woman sleeps, the Aparecido gives her pleasure and she keeps liking it."

"I'd suggest that we put one spell on her clothes and another on her body," Pilar said.

"A holy cross made from the bone of a dog, to protect her clothes. Put a holy cross in her suitcase. A rosary should be made from dried black-eyed peas with a green scapular. That way the Aparecido won't be able to get inside her and travel with her."

Tía Cecilia arrived in New York with the rosary around her neck and a list of young ladies' residences that Project Oz had provided her with. She stayed with the great-aunts for a few days and they took the rosary from around her neck: "It's not fashionable," they declared.

The great-aunts surprised their guest with a trousseau of Chanel clothing that they had bought at a used clothing sale from a rich Jewish woman. They opened the suitcase to put the trousseau in and found a cross made from the bone of a dog and a green scapular with the Prayer of the Powerful Hand. "Child, this isn't used in Madrid. You have to get used to the style, the tone of that city."

23

Cecilia arrived in Madrid tired and sleepy one misty night. She wore a tailored two-piece Chanel suit of green wool with matching shoes. The great-aunts had prepared her with a hot cup of cannabis tea so that Tía Cecilia would not get motion sick on the flight, but as we all know, cannabis can cause tiredness and sleepiness. Once she was in Madrid, Tía Cecilia could scarcely bear her exhaustion. With great difficulty she took from her handbag the paper with the names of two young ladies' residences, took a taxi, and reached the first digs. A fat woman who smelled like garlic, wearing a dirty apron, showed her the rooms. Tía Cecilia, being so tired and sleepy, chose the first room she saw. It wasn't bad. A room with floral wallpaper, a four-poster bed, a bookcase, and sink. The bathroom was at the end of the hall.

Tía Cecilia dropped her suitcases, said good-bye to the fat woman, and threw herself on the bed still wearing her Chanel outfit. She slept for three days, and for three days the fat woman would stop in the hallway to yell, "Girl! Are you still alive in there?"

Tía Cecilia dreamed of an Aparecido who flies at midnight and his guts go in and out of people who sleep with their mouths open. Then he gets inside women and kisses their darkest parts. The woman feels comfortable and keeps liking it.

On the third day, she woke up and took a long shower and the fat woman yelled, "Girl! Why so long in the bath?"

At the School of Medicine in the city of Madrid, Tía Cecilia supported herself for two years on her savings and the money that Felipe sent her. On some afternoons, when she had some free time, she would go out to explore the city. ¡Viva España! ¡Viva el Ejército! ¡Viva Franco! were the only signs you could see throughout that city of winding streets, antiquated hostels, taverns, bars, inns, and cafes. Tía Cecilia became just another transient and in her Chanel suit she wandered through museums, antique bookstores, plazas, newsstands, cafes done up in the fashionable "Belle Epoque" style, terraces, and bars. One of those afternoons she was approached by a man with intense eyes and hair shiny with Brylcreem. That first meeting led to dates in the parks and bars of Madrid. Then they were seen walking hand-in-hand along the narrow streets around the student housing.

They decided to share their joy in the surrounding areas and traveled to Toledo, loving each other in the stone corners of the amphitheatre at Covachuelas. In Segovia they spent afternoons charmed by the landscape with its castles and the place's clean air. At San Lorenzo del Escorial, that granite mass, they traversed its halls in silence, holding hands. For months, nightfall found them in the middle of some plaza, forced to stay in some obscure lodging in the town, which my aunt used her savings to pay for. Not long after, the couple decided to live together in Tía Cecilia's little room with the money that Felipe continued to send to his sister studying medicine in Spain.

After six months, the man proposed. "I need to finish school. And what would we live on?" asked Tía Cecilia.

"What are you talking about? My family owns properties and I live off the rents, and furthermore, I manage those properties."

It might seem strange to you, but Tía Cecilia was convinced by that man with oiled hair, and after verifying that his documents were in order, they were married in a little parish near the center of Madrid.

"Now you know, you are married, my child. Never again shall you oppose your husband, nor talk back to him, nor go against him. You shall remain silent and with your head down, you shall give into everything, no matter what happens. Woman was made to bear man's blows, rage, and whims," the priest pronounced.

When they left the church, the town crier, from the balcony of the bakery in the town square, was giving the speech of St. Isidore. Tía Cecilia, overwhelmed by her joy, looked up at the blue sky of that hamlet and understood the saying "De Madrid al cielo y algún agujerito para verlo": from Madrid to Heaven, all you need is a little hole to see it.

The voice of the preacher rang out shrilly:

"Madrileños by birth, by work, or by choice; outsiders, foreigners, tramps, and transients: ¡Viva Madrid, which is and should be the home of all, and viva San Isidro Labrador, patron of contemplative loafers and celestial foreman of freelance day-laboring angels! ¡Viva my owner! said the baker's wide belly and so did the blade of the bloodcurdling goat-shearing knife that is also used to cut up chorizo for lunch," et cetera, et cetera.

24

[Rain, rain, go away, come again some other day.] Early one February morning, two tourists from Denver were enjoying a long walk on the beach. When they reached the rocky outcrop, the man and his girlfriend sat down on the sand moistened by the waves. The ocean beat its waves against the shore at the outcropping, the smell of salt was sharp, and the pelicans flew furiously over the waves. It took them a few seconds to focus their sights on the distance.

"It's probably just a big fish."

"I don't think so."

A bundle was approaching the shore and the couple stood up, brushed the sand from their knees, and walked over to it. And thus they discovered that corpse floating toward the shore. They walked out until they could reach its neck and pulled the body up onto the dry sand. That beach was surrounded by a few summer houses abandoned by their owners in the last hurricane. People had taken advantage of the owners' departure and torn out windows, doors, shelving, and wardrobes by their roots. All that was left were simple cement shells that smelled of old urine and rotting sea-flesh. That's where the tourist couple went to take shelter from the wave of police officers, captains, detectives, and journalists.

That morning everyone awoke to a brilliant sun and cloudless sky. Pilar went into the kitchen where Felipe was making fried eggs with bacon and pan criollo, she opened the porch door and breathed the morning air. A few sheets of glass that decorated the roof of the porch banged together in the wind. Every morning Pilar walked along the seashore and half an hour later would be walking back along the coast. Far off, she could make out a dark stain in the sky. A downpour was coming. Two fat old seagulls were flying over the coastline. Pilar looked up and noticed the commotion. "What's going on?"

"They found a body. A drowning. Go find out."

It was noon when Pilar got back to her house. She had stopped at the grocer's, the pharmacy, and the bakery. When she arrived, she saw Minerva sitting on the front steps. As soon as Minerva saw Pilar, she rushed over to her, hugged her hard, and said, "I have bad news for you."

"Who died?"

"Cecilia is dead. That fucking Spaniard. He stabbed her. The bastard! The great-aunts are bringing the body this afternoon. Felipe and Fernando have already left for the airport."

"I figured something terrible would happen. This morning I saw a corpse on the beach, and that's an ill omen."

The wood of the coffin that held Tía Cecilia's remains was of the finest white almond wood. Rather than a corpse, the coffin gave the impression that it held a treasure trove of diamonds and pearls. It was placed in the grandparents' parlor. The great-aunts gave instructions to close the shutters and prohibited conversation in normal voices. The grandparents did not cry; they held and consoled each other quietly in a constant murmur, so as not to wake Tía Cecilia from the sleep of the dead. Minerva and Fernando wrung their hands, and Claudia Luz and Felipe consoled each other as best they could in a corner.

Pilar walked in circles around the coffin, trying to understand the story that passed from mouth to mouth, as she tried to recognize Tía Cecilia with her black hair and grayish skin, too gray for our tropical sun. Pilar tried over and over to reconstruct the story like a jigsaw puzzle with missing pieces, without understanding how that animal could have stabbed my Tía Cecilia seventeen times. Pilar wanted to find a deep forest in the middle of an ordinary night and mourn for the loss of my Tía Cecilia, she wanted to find answers about such a senseless death, and she wanted to know more about the murderer, the executioner. "Tell me, Felipe, do they know anything about the husband?"

"Yes. I contacted the Madrid police. They've caught him and they'll sentence him to hang, like in the old days."

"Make sure they do."

"Don't worry."

Felipe sat on the floor and rested his head in his wife's lap and, without saying anything more, cried as he had never cried before. The sadness that lived in the grandparents' house in those days floated like a wounded balloon filled with contaminated air. The pain in everyone's eyes burned like a dull ax in the middle of your chest; but the worst part was that the women in that family discovered what terror was, that cold dungeon full of scorpions. For a long time there was no consoling prayer, no elevated spirit, no rose-scented nymph that could raise my family's mood, except for the cannabis tea that the great-aunts made. As part of their healing arts, the great-aunts decided to put a little bit of cannabis in the beans that they cooked every day. They had a great deal of faith in the healing capacity of this plant. They also mixed seeds of the plant with the sugar they put in the morning coffee. In this way, the family was able to rest from the terror and the agony of pain without the dark witches of death stalking the house.

A few days after the burial, we decided to clean out the family pantheon. We found it there in the middle of the dried herbs and shyleaf between a cave of centipedes and a puddle of mud. This One and That One scrubbed the colorless little wall with a brush, and the bronze tablet was traced out with pure adoration. Now that so many years have passed, the only thing I remember is the soft light of the lamps and the opulent coffin. I can't remember the color of my aunt's hair anymore, but I do remember the scent of the infinite sea the day she was buried. A few old women that no one knew attended the burial. One of them threw a cross made from the bone of a dog into the hole. No one knew them except Pilar, Claudia Luz, and me.

"Old women, who are you? What are you doing here? What did you throw into the tomb?" Minerva screamed.

"They are the witches of the Caño. The ones that make dolls and throw them into the Caño in a wooden box. The ones that plunder the cemetery in search of the bones of the dead, locks of hair, old teeth, fingernails, or a piece of shroud. The ones that grind up the bones of the skull and hairs from the mane and tail of a horse. The ones that wrap up lovers' whispers in plantain leaves. The ones that put spells on the rafters of houses, on the balconies, or on the stairs so that the foundation of your life falls apart," answered That One.

25

When the meteorologists announced the storm, Felipe was traveling through Central America. It wasn't the first time that Pilar had gone through a storm in that house without Felipe. In the last meteorological phenomenon, the wind knifed through the shutters and panes of glass until it whipped through our house. I remember the creaking of the ceiling lights. The pictures banged loudly against the walls, and the table ornaments shattered against the floor. I held myself rigid, squeezed tightly into my room. The lights disappeared and since the windows remained shut, we were in the dark all night.

Hurricanes are formed in the warm waters right on the equator. When the sun shines with full force on those lands and seas, every centimeter of the planet heats in the same ratio. The sea boils, and great quantities of water evaporate and produce a huge bomb of energy. The winds, sand, and dust of the Sahara push the water vapor to produce a whirlwind, a spiral that spins and spins like Pilar's head. The eye of the storm forms and that's when humans and birds are imprisoned in that transparent cage.

That hurricane brought so much rain that the ground was saturated and the valleys ended up with all the earth of the mountains. Animals that were trapped in the mud ended up slamming against the rocky outcroppings of those mountains. The cows, horses, dogs, and pigs drowned, their bladders swollen. The hurricane covered the whole island with its seas, and everything turned a uniform shade of gray.

I go out into the hallway and see Pilar's feet. She is walking back and forth with a flashlight. The light throws enormous shadows like Chinese shadow puppets. Her feet look gigantic. Pilar goes from room to room checking the windows. Sometimes she appears through the doors that lead out onto the terrace. The wind blows so hard that the coconut palms look like ancient pipe cleaners, and the other trees bend as the wind blows.

"Are you all right?" Pilar has come into my room, she has asked me how I am.

"Yes, I'm fine; don't worry about me."

Pilar took her pill and went to bed wearing her street clothes and everything else. I curled up in bed and covered myself with the sheets. That night we had a visitation. The Aparecido visited us. Pilar's flashlight showed him in full body. You could see his transparent figure observing Pilar's movements. What did he come for? I could find no answer because the fear I felt that night left my brain addled. I wanted to shout to Pilar, Watch out, Mami! But my mother didn't realize. The Aparecido followed her footsteps throughout the house. She was overcome with shivering, but imagined that it was because of the wind slipping between the slats of the shutters. I stayed mute, silent, immobile, incapable of any movement. For a long time I couldn't sense Pilar, either. I don't know how long I spent in the solitude of my room. The wind was deafening. My fear was so great that I thought my heart would turn to stone. For several minutes I gathered my courage, and then got up and walked to Pilar's room. I couldn't find her. I looked through the whole house; I don't know where she was. I called, "Mami, Mami!"

I couldn't find her. I went into her room once again and noticed the
Book of Mediums on her bed. I picked it up and curled up on the
bed. Sleep overcame me suddenly, as if someone had covered me
with a cloud of dust. When the sun came up, everything was over.
The hurricane had moved on to Hispaniola; it would go across the
north of Cuba and turn to Jamaica. Pilar came into the room and
woke me up. She was surrounded by a halo of happiness. For some
inexplicable reason she looked rested and relaxed. "What do you
want for breakfast?" she asked me.

"Oatmeal and juice," I answered.

Pilar left the room and I remembered the book. I looked for it
and found that it had a page marked. I opened it to that page:

> Imagine that a soul that has reached the level of perfection
> may no longer need its corporeal organs in order to act. In
> effect, acting by sheer will, it is evident that it can do without
> the body. This is what happens with magnetism, and in many
> other cases whenever a violent passion is manifested and
> works on its assistants, independent of direct, immediate com-
> munication. So for example, the magnetizer is able to cause a
> subject on which he is acting to sleepwalk even when the sub-
> ject is far away, without even touching the subject. Thus there
> is an independent manifestation of corporeal action, physical
> touch, material communication. And it is not unlikely that a
> man who has isolated his animate essence and purified it suffi-
> ciently to manifest himself independent of his body, preserves
> the ability to manifest in this way after the destruction of the
> body. But few spirits are capable of raising themselves to the
> level of perfection necessary to reach this goal.

Three days later, I was swinging on the swings with Minerva in
what was left of the park. Most of the swings had been torn out
by their roots and dangled from almond and tamarind trees. The
old trees surrounding the area remained standing with a few
broken and twisted branches. Minerva and I contemplated the
wondrous splendor of the emerald green color of the sea.

"Do you want to walk over to the house with the taxidermy animals, Titi Minerva?"

We went. We entered the museum, and as always, not a soul was there. The animals, stuffed full of cotton and natural fibers, looked at us with glassy eyes, motionless. Rabbits, owls, Bengal tigers, deer, eagles, butterflies on wires, sharks, and swordfish living together with their cohorts. They have remained in the same position for years. The smell of old meat filled the premises.

"Did the hurricane frighten you?"

"Yes, a lot."

"And wasn't Pilar there with you?"

"We were in the living room together, but then we went to our own rooms. What I do know is that the Aparecido visited us that night, and the next day my mother got news of Bella Juncos's death."

26

[Tell me why, tell me why do fools fall in love? Tell me why, oh, oh why do fools fall in love?] The famous poet Bella Juncos was born in a deserted lot in the town of Humacao as her mother was walking down to the river to do laundry. Her mother screamed, and a group of neighbor women ran to help her. Her parents were Julia Santiago and José María Cruz. Bella's childhood was a typical rural childhood. Her mother took her to the river every day, specifically to a pool behind the house. There she learned to swim, and like a fish in water she spent afternoons and evenings in that spot or dangling like a monkey, hunting through the branches of the mango trees along the bank of the river until one day her grandmother said, "Mija, it's time you began school." She was enrolled in several public schools in the Julián Blanco section of Fajardo, and when she became a young lady, her family moved to Río Piedras. Her mother, doña Julia, managed a rooming house, and her father, don José María, made pastries and coconut sweets for restaurants and coffee shops. Bella entered the Escuela Normal of the Universidad de Puerto Rico and completed a certificate as a master seamstress. She never finished a single dress, since her time was devoted to reading and writing poetry, but in any case, in those days she was seen on strike with the sewing workers in Mayagüez, where she argued with them about dialectical materialism, and she was also present for the general seamstresses' strike that was declared in Ponce. There she was seen with a group of university students passing out political propaganda. In 1951 she worked in Comerío, Adjuntas, and Barranquitas as a Department of Agriculture employee at a "milk station," passing out breakfasts to poor children. She was, in under a year, married to and divorced from Jacinto Diáfano Paredes, as the latter impregnated another woman. The people of the neighborhood saw the woman walking by with her child and said, "She really has her father's face."

After finalizing her divorce, Bella moved to San Juan and worked as an office assistant in the store belonging to Mr. Gautier, the mayor's husband. It was there that she met Pilar, who would become one of her greatest friends. About that time, she published her first book. Since in those days there were no "how to publish your own books" manuals, she was forced to bust her brain in a print shop trying to understand what goes first; if it's verse or reverse, the photo or the introduction. She took advantage of her lunch hour to place her book of poetry in the drugstores and newsstands of Old San Juan. On weekends she would take public transportation to the nearby towns to place her books in different businesses. At night she was frequently seen at meetings of sugar cane workers and protests of public transportation drivers. Besides her reputation as a nationalist, by this time her reputation as a femme fatale had begun to follow her as she fell into countless romances.

Her poetry became well known both on and off the island. Her pictures began to appear frequently in the culture pages of the newspapers. Over the years, the better-known photographs of the famous poetess became well known. Look: Bella at the reading of one of her poems at the Ateneo. Bella at the Social Civic Club of Cabo Rojo. Bella behind a table with several of her published books of poetry. Bella with a group of the city's intellectuals. Bella on a horse at Álvaro Mujica's estate. Bella reading Baudelaire's poetry for a distinguished public. Bella visiting don Pedro in jail. In the picture you can see him taking her hand. Kissing her fingers. These last pictures gave rise to speculation. Soon she traveled to Havana following a Dominican intellectual who was visiting the island. The Cuban press commented on the large number of recitals, public events, and social dinners in which Bella participated. At one of those events she met Pablo Neruda, and the poet said, "Bella, I think I have a poem that is very similar to one of yours, the one that begins, 'Little rose, at times tiny and naked, you fit in my hand . . .'" and she answered him, "How curious, don Pablo, we poets are so far apart and yet so close together." About that time, exactly where is unknown, the famous poet Juan Ramón Jiménez, upon being asked in an interview, "Do you know Bella Juncos?", replied, "Of course . . . poor thing . . . She has some lovely poems . . ." The famed poet treated his wife Zenobia with the same compassion when he saw her carrying all his briefcases, papers, manuscripts, and books. He looked at his wife with the unique consternation that a master shows toward his slave, saying, "Poor little thing, she works so hard." The rumors that Bella Juncos was unwell increased. What's wrong with Bella? An extended press release by the Havana *Diario la Marina* may be able to give us the answer.

> Bella Juncos, the well-known poetess, began a relationship some time ago with a prominent Dominican, one of the foremost exile leaders and the son of a high-society family. Fleeing from the aforementioned's family, they took a boat to Havana, where the couple joined the upper spheres of Dominican political exiles. Bella enrolled in the Universidad de la Habana and immediately attracted the attention of her classmates and intellectual circles of the city. Taking advantage of an occasion when her consort had to make a trip to Venezuela, Ms. Juncos entertained herself with another political leader: the one with light eyes and a calm gaze, and was seen walking

arm-in-arm with him toward Plaza de la Catedral late one night. By coincidence, that individual was also Dominican. There must be something about Dominicans! Upon his return, her companion was informed upon by a political comrade and boom! Bella was abandoned in a second-rate hotel without a cent and had to borrow money in order to leave the country. That was how a few friends helped her to make her way to New York. The act caused commotion not only within the intellectual circles of Havana, Santo Domingo, and San Juan, but also caused one of the strongest Dominican organizations in exile to split in half, and all over a bit of skirt.

Did our famous poet die in a sanatorium, there in the cold cement up north, or at the corner of 103rd and Fifth Avenue? In literary circles, it is said that a young Nuyorican poet saw her a few days before her death. It was exactly twelve noon on a clear spring day. The Nuyorican was eating a hot dog, sitting on a bench next to two old women who were smoking cannabis and laughing like teenagers. The Nuyorican confused the famous poet with a homeless person, and the old women assured him, "She cannot be homeless; she's that famous Puerto Rican poet." Bella died that same spring. Through the efforts of a group of her friends, she was brought back to the island. Her burial will be remembered for years. Her wake was held in the Catedral de San Juan, and her body was viewed by dignitaries and intellectuals who fought over who would appear in the official photo. Her close friend Pilar attended the wake, accompanied by her husband, Felipe. There has been a lot of speculation about the longtime friendship between those two women, but little is known. They worked together in a store in Old San Juan, and were often seen walking through the streets together. Pilar, the distinguished wife of an upper-level executive on the island, appeared at the viewing in a fashionable tropical-cut dress that left half her back exposed. Her long hair and her finely-drawn red lips deposited a kiss on the deceased's forehead. The poetess's remains repose at Cementerio de Villa Palmeras in tomb number 143.

BELLA'S FINAL LETTER TO HER MOTHER

April 7, 1956

Dear Mother,

Although you haven't known this, I must confess that I have rather given myself over to drink. So much so that the doctors have diagnosed me with cirrhosis of the liver. Your last letter has confronted me. I am sick, not just in the body but in the soul. In your letter you give me recipes for potions and witches' herbs that I wouldn't be able to find here. Life is a golden roulette or a castle within another castle, as St. Theresa said. She said in the sixteenth century (though I believe it was really Nawadir who said it) that for each son of Adam, God built seven castles, in the center of which He is, and outside of which Satan is barking like a dog. When man allows a breach to open in one of those castles, Beelzebub enters. You will say it's spirits without the capacity for reason. Every castle is made of a precious stone. The first castle is made of pearl, and inside it there is a castle of emerald, inside of which is a castle of porcelain, inside of which is a castle of stone, inside of which is a castle of iron, inside of which is a castle of gold. I believe that my castles have been falling apart little by little, and all that is left to me is the castle of words, which Nawadir never mentioned. At this point I can no longer distract myself with magic recipes or witches' cauldrons. I am a combatant who has now surrendered in the face of so many secrets.

Poetry and you are always in my thoughts.

In your world, with devotion,

Bella

27

In the summer Felipe and Fernando would take a two-propeller airplane from the Isla Grande airport to Martinique to fish for tuna, sawfish, red snapper, and mahi-mahi, because fishing at that latitude was strengthened by the winds and the depths. From the little airplane you could see all the islands surrounded by white beaches and deep blue seas. As you descend, you see little groups of wooden huts with straw and tin roofs; you can make out minuscule roads, together with imaginary lines of coconut palms and cultivated fields of sugarcane. On the coast the brothers rented a boat, the *Miss Paulette*, near the rows of yoles rondes, the boats decorated by the island's natives in bright reds, yellows, greens. A cooler full of ice and rhum agricole, the rum of the island, promised good fishing, and bamboo oars promised a return in case the boat's motor died.

Felipe and Fernando were also aficionados of the blue marlin fishing tournament sponsored by the Nautical Club. They traveled the northern coast in a little boat owned by one of Felipe's business partners. They dropped lines with bait of pieces of shrimp and

red snapper until they caught their prey. For marlin fishing they
would leave early in the morning. Those were days of excitement,
enthusiasm, and hard work. Although hard work was something
incomprehensible to Felipe, who got bored with holding the fishing
rods, he entertained himself by making martinis and Cuba libres,
or beating eggs to mix with flour to make fried breem over a little
gas stove. On other occasions they took the harpoon and lay in wait
for the barracudas that approached the boat in search of food. The
north of the island has hundreds of beaches, millions of grains of
sand: white, pink, cream, and gray. An enormous amount of sea-
weed and snails washes up on the shore, and huge lobsters live in
the water, which is colored by thousands of tropical fish and coral
reefs. In the distance, you can make out a handful of floating houses
when the wind over the ocean calms and rows of small wood palaces with wide marble steps stretch from the water to the sky.

Fernando spends hours on the shores of those coasts. He
swims out to the nearest cape, stretches out on the whitish sand,
and observes closely the little fish in the clear water as well as the
human scenery on the horizon.

Fernando must have been about twenty-one when he became
known as a singer. He imitated the most popular singers while listening to the radio stations on the military bases. He was especially
intrigued by the secret of falsetto in the voices of U.S. blacks. In
the afternoons, he walked along the beach harmonizing with the
birds, especially the turtledoves, and often sang a duo with them.
The birds gaped at him, amazed to have such a human companion.
Fernando's passion was music, and the motor of his life, rhythm.
[Fernando gorrioncillo, pecho amarillo.]

"Did you know I enlisted in the army?"

"Yes. The folks told me. What are you going to do there,
bro', you know you don't have to go. I can get you a job," Felipe
answered him.

"No, brother, thank you. I want to leave, and I think the army
is a good opportunity, but don't worry, I'll come back and be really
famous."

"Fernando, the only thing I ask is that you be careful. The folks couldn't stand another tragedy," Felipe replied.

It was very hard for the grandparents to accept that Fernando was also leaving them, but he did. After three months of military training, he auditioned to be part of the entertainment show organized for the soldiers, and for two years he traveled from fort to fort entertaining the troops with a group of singing soldiers. That's why the family says, "Fernando salió cantando del army: he came out of the army singing." Once he finished his military service, my uncle decided to live in New York. Within the Boricua community they organized trios and quartets, groups that vocalized among themselves and exchanged songs, and [Que me toquen Las golondrinas.] Fernando became part of this core of musicians and singers that moved throughout the city.

One day in the middle of a winter like any other, one of the great-aunts was making hot chocolate. She was listening to Radio WADO, her favorite station while mixing milk and a bar of Cortés chocolate in a saucepan. Add cinnamon, a little bit of sugar, and keep stirring until the chocolate begins to melt. Yum, delicious! As we were saying, one of the great-aunts was listening to the radio. The deejay announced the magnificent recording by a group of boys from right here in El Barrio, East Harlem, and anyone who doesn't know by now what and where El Barrio is, they really don't know what's what! Since El Barrio is where one of the beating hearts of the Boricua community in New York is anchored, the main puertorro heartbeat of Manhattan. We were talking about those boys who had just recorded their first 45 with the famous bolero "Comprende Que Mi Corazón" . . . and we won't talk anymore, my compatriots; I will leave you with the boys.

The deejay said all this, and Fernando's first recording was heard on the radio. [Cucurrucucú, paloma.] The aunt thought she heard a very familiar voice and called the radio station, confirming that it really was her nephew who had recorded a 45, and not a flight of fancy due to the cannabis. [Excuse me, could you please play "Que me toquen Las golondrinas."] She immediately notified the family in a letter.

Fernando worked as a dishwasher, waiter, barber, and cook. Once he worked in a funeral parlor and decided to collect all the hooks from the flowers that were put on the dead people's tombs, filling all of the funeral parlor's cupboards with them, which caused scarcity in the city. He resold them at a better price and used the money for his music business. Who says that stuff about supply and demand doesn't work? On weekends he sang in bars and cabarets, and late at night he walked down to the basements in Harlem where the blacks composed and sang blues. They were little bars decorated with floral garlands and colored lights and a platform in the back. In one of those little jukebox joints, or translated to Castilian, a ratonera de cantazo, around 2:00 a.m., individuals began to parade in dressed in wide hats, jackets down to their ankles, and brilliantly colored neckties, and were carrying all kinds of musical instruments. The female singers would arrive later, take off all the deceptions they had put on to fight the cold, and go into the bathroom to touch up their hair and makeup. On the stage, a lit cigarette would light up their neck and show their lips and nails painted a glowing red: [Don't the sun look lonesome setting down behind the trees? Don't your house look lonesome when your baby's packed to leave?]

With his head full of plans, Fernando announced his return to Puerto Rico. When Fernando saw from the sky El Morro rising from the island and the raging waves singing against the beach, he felt satisfied and in a state of benediction. When the plane landed, the passengers' massive applause confirmed to him that this is where I want to be. I want to make it clear that the applause was not in honor of Fernando, but rather the fact that we arrived safe and sound, damn it!

The receiving committee at the airport was made up of sisters, nieces, nephews, and his brother Felipe. The greetings, laughter, and voices of everyone were too much, and made him remember where he was. His mother and father back at home were waiting for him with loving embraces, and as God commands, a good lobster asopao. Everyone talked simultaneously while the laughter in the air mixed with the noise of the neighborhood. Abuelo Cristóbal opened bottles and distributed aromatic liqueurs; yet at times Fernando felt that he was still walking with his friends down the dark streets of New York. All of this was a dream. At any moment he would wake up.

"What are you planning on doing now?" Felipe asked, pulling him aside from the hubbub.

"I'm going to continue my career as a singer."

"Listen, everybody, my little brother is going to continue his career as a singer. That's what we need, someone famous in the family."

With his savings and help from the grandparents, Fernando took voice lessons. His teacher couldn't classify her student's voice definitively: "Maybe you're a baritone. You have a voice that hasn't yet been modified by adulthood. Maybe you'll end up as a tenor."

In order to keep his vocal cords healthy, he swallowed a raw egg yolk every morning and gargled with rosewater.

"Intonation, Fernando, intonation is important, and don't forget that there is no limit to resonance."

On that corner he did vocal exercises with two guys from the neighborhood who also wanted to be singers.

"The neck extended, the mouth open in a circle, the nose fully ready to receive and expel air."

The teacher and her student manipulated the voice by paraphrasing long, complicated sentences.

"Tone, you should modulate your tone, because men have a tone that's more explosive, more muscular. That causes difficulty in the pronunciation of words and phrases."

In the afternoons he kept practicing his vocal exercises with those two guys. The group harmonized so well that they decided to form a trio.

"Can you give classes to these two also?"

"Not for the price of one. Each of you must pay me separately."

In my grandparents' living room the group prepared several fashionable rhythms, rehearsing for months in front of an audience of young people who gathered around the porch. They finally had their opportunity, a debut on the aficionado program on Radio WKAQ, causing a great sensation. Overnight the group's popularity grew like weeds. In five months' time, the group was heard in Panama and throughout the Caribbean, thanks to short-wave radios and the innumerable sailors who went from port to port carrying packs filled with 45s. [Cucurrucucú paloma] Soon afterwards, the group prepared their songs and was able to record their first LP. The record sold like hotcakes, and this led the sponsors of radio stations in the Dominican Republic to invite them to Ciudad Trujillo, the land most loved by Columbus. [Ahí viene el gato y el ratón, a darle combate al tiburón.]

The Santo Domingo airport was in immense disorder: people talking in shouts and carrying boxes, bundles, and rucksacks, mixed with musicians on the corner who, in order to earn some coins, would sit down to play merengue ripiao with drums and güiros. A driver was waiting for them to take them to La Voz Dominicana, where a famous radio promoter received for them with open arms. That night on the stage of a fashionable hotel, the trio premiered their show before a large audience of generals wearing sabers and epaulets with their distinguished wives. The box-office record that the boys established could hardly be equaled. Never before had so many people been seen at the hotel. [Que me toquen Las golondrinas] The line at the entrance seemed endless. What you must realize is that they had not yet been invited to appear in any films.

When the show ended, the group was invited by one of El Chivo's sons to the *Victoria*, anchored at Boca Chica. Among the guests of honor were some officials of Pérez Jiménez's government and a certain lady who was a delegate of the American Institute of Democracy. The dock was full of undercover police and military barriers, always at the ready. Great quantities of whiskey, rum, and El Presidente beer were served, along with a paella seasoned with the famous beer that was the centerpiece of the buffet. That turned out to be a spectacular party. The next morning El Chivo's sons and his friends, completely drunk, fired the high-caliber cannons of the boat. It was one of the many jokes that El Jefe's son played. The row that ensued was so great that the trio had to hide in the captain's berth and later leave escorted by American military police, together with the lady who was the delegate for the American Institute of Democracy. Believe it or not, this episode increased the popularity of the group. They accepted countless invitations to travel all over the Caribbean, Central America, and Europe. New York was always a necessary stop because the audience, señores y señoras, loved them. Every time the group visited New York, they managed to break new records. [WOW!!! Now that's what I call a show!!!]

28

By now, Fernando had countless working relationships with other singers and musicians, especially with the bolero singers who sing of love or betrayal, invoking the shadow of passion, accompanied by guitars and maracas, or accompanied by big bands, in audacious and intensely provocative outfits. "En la vida hay amores que nunca pueden olvidarse, imborrables momentos que siempre guarda el corazón." He met all the flamenco guitarists who had come over from the motherland, thin and addicted to opium, who sang qué bonitos ojos tienes debajo de esas dos cejas, debajo de esas dos cejas malagueña salerosa ¡¡¡Viva España!!! ¡¡¡Que viva España gloriosa!!! They ended every song that way, just like the Mexicans, except that the Mexicans shouted, "¡Va por México! ¡Que viva México, hijos de la chingada!" Fernando was courted by the zarzuela singers and groups of minstrels from Madrid who were docked in the port of San Juan while on tour through the Americas. The zarzuela singers were matronly women with large tits and flowers in their hair who gave off a sensual sweat. On the other hand, the boys of the minstrel groups seemed like they had come from a cheap porcelain factory.

Each and every one was invited to my grandparents' living room, where long musical conversations took place. Abuela María, busy as a beaver, prepared oyster asopao and fresh chicken for the guests' consumption. Abuelo Cristóbal arrived with packages of Serrano ham and Spanish chorizo, which is the best (not Mexican chorizo, which is just an imitation). He did his best to ensure that there was always a good amount of imported liquor and sugar rum from the stills in the Caño. Felipe and Minerva always showed off their skills as excellent hosts. They went from guest to guest carrying samples of ron caña, clandestine rum in little crystal glasses, and passing out cups of foreign liquors.

Pilar, especially, felt a deep admiration for the bolero singers, and whenever a musical soirée was announced, she did her best to be there. We will now describe Pilar's wardrobe for the viewing audience. Comfortably dressed, that lovely citizen of our capital wears white capri pants and a coordinating checked blouse or perhaps a flowered cotton suit and matching sandals. Take note, my dear ladies. Pilar was always punctual. She would sit in a corner of the room while she opened her fan with the black ribs. She loved to spy on the bolero singers' audacity and provocativeness. Listening to these women sing, my mother learned to perfect the art of pretense and pretending, and to hide desire beneath an instinctual mask. Furthermore, by studying the boleristas' songs, she discovered the enigma of the perfect wife and prayed to the forces of the universe to be an apt pupil of each of those women. [¡Agúzate, mi negra!]

Tía Minerva was in charge of controlling the crowd that begged admittance to the grandparents' house every time the trio rehearsed. She was in her element opening and closing the front door to whomever she felt like; she winked at all the musicians, singers, and boleristas she found interesting, and showed her rear to every attractive businessman who had money. People loved Minerva's flair and taste. On Saturday afternoons, after having slept the amanecida, she would go to Santurce to buy records and arrive with the latest from the hit parade. On Sundays she helped Abuelo Cristóbal organize the liquor that arrived in contraband shipments from Venezuela, Mexico, and Panama.

Abuelo Cristóbal had a warehouse near the Caño that had previously been a toothpaste factory. Three fans cooled the air. Although Abuelo Cristóbal now had the means to legalize his business, he had discovered that there is no better way to carry out commercial transactions than via speculation and illegal trafficking. It was a business uncomplicated by the payment of taxes or customs. He had built an empire, and he wasn't about to let it go down the drain in the name of democratic concessions. These sales had enabled him to obtain a factory that made sacks, another that made bottles, and a tire-retreading plant, and he placated the government by paying the taxes on those three products. It was the time of the Alliance for Progress and of doña Inés and her two ugly daughters. Abuelo Cristóbal was the best liquor supplier in the country, and Tía Minerva, with time, became an expert in liquors. The bartender, you could say. There she refined her knowledge of American whiskey, cordials, brandy, beers, gins, vodkas, rums, crèmes, tequilas, frappés, highballs, hot drinks, juleps, Pernod, pousse-cafés, punches, Triple Secs, wines, liquors, Campari, angostura, anisettes, apéritifs, Crème de Cassis, Curaçao, digestifs, grenadines, madeiras, ports, "on the rocks" for the Americans, Pisco for the young ladies, sherry for the Americans, rum, rum, watch out he's drunk, don't let him leave without paying, rum, rum, rum, rum, extra rocks, white rum, gold rum, sweet Jamaica rum, cane rum, molasses rum, pitorro rum.

The cocktail hour. The moment when the work hours have been left behind and the leisure hours have begun. The elegant men of our capital city in casual clothes enjoyed themselves:

"Minerva, I'm having a party at my house; give me a couple of good recipes for cocktails."

"That's easy. An ounce of rum, half an ounce of gin, a quarter ounce of lemon, two to three ounces of Coca-Cola. Cuba libre, rum and Coke.

"Half an ounce of rum, three-quarters of an ounce of lemon, three-quarters of an ounce of syrup. Shake with crushed ice. Daiquiri.

"One ounce Campari, half an ounce of vermouth, soda water. Americano.

"Half an ounce of tequila, 3/4 oz. Crème de Cacao, 1/2 oz. lemon. Diablo."

[Échele amigo nomás échele y llene hasta el borde la copa de champán.]

29

I would go into Tía Minerva's room and sit on her bed,
I would watch her get dressed   get undressed,
        open drawers,
close drawers,
change her hairstyle ten times a day,
        come out of the room,
come into the room.
We would curl up in her bed to take our siesta,
Close together,
joined,
with me,
with her,
me sleeping together with her.
The two of us mixed
together in an embrace
and one dream for both of us.

Crossing a wide marsh in the darkness. The night birds had stopped chirping, the mangrove swamp was deserted. Minerva leads me by the hand as she points: there in the distance, that transparent man with the clear, sad look in his eyes, his bearing dull but caring. He transports himself, reaches us, opens his mouth, and throws up hundreds of rotten worms. Tía Minerva dreams that the night birds have stopped chirping and the mangrove swamp is deserted.

At that moment, the bedroom was a conglomerate of souls and Eusapia Palladino moved right into my heart: "My child, my child." I was sleeping, and was able to keep dreaming of Eusapia Palladino passing out holy water and transparent aromas. "My child, my child," she repeated.

Without moving her lips, Eusapia Palladino touched my cheek without touching me,
without feeling me,
without feeling her,
until the sun took over the room.

I awoke because of the heat and the spirits shrieked, scorched by the high temperatures, melting their energy away in front of me. I took stock of the room: the dresser, the closet, the bed, the pictures on the wall, all the objects in my room. Everything was in its place. I was almost a child, almost a woman. Almost a woman.

"What did you dream about?"
"About an Aparecido. You?"
"I don't know, about a man, but you were in the dream too."

Minerva gets up and goes to the window. She has seen someone she knows. [Testing. Testing. One, two, three o'clock, four o'clock, rock.] She goes to the mirror, runs a comb through her hair, puts on lipstick and goes out to the street. She goes down the stairs, [five, six, seven o'clock, twelve o'clock, rock] walks toward a group of guys on the corner and a man approaches her. Minerva strokes his face. [We're gonna rock around the clock tonight] She kisses him on the mouth and they move away from the group. They walk slowly out of the neighborhood and reach one of the most imposing houses up on the hill. The man rests a hand on Minerva's rear and *bam!* se la llevó pa'l monte. [One, two, three o'clock, four o'clock, rock. Five, six, seven o'clock, rock.] He stops and takes a key from his pocket and they tiptoe onto the terrace filled with doves. They undress with a naturality born of familiarity and make love under the stars to the sound of the doves' cooing.

By this time, my dear readers, Minerva was one of the greatest hookers in the neighborhood and well-honored for it.

"Have you seen Minerva?" Abuela María asked.

"She must have gone to bed," Abuelo Juan answered.

"But I saw her go downstairs."

"Then she must have gone back up."

[Sum, sum, sum, sum sum Babaé.] There in the Caño, the old women crouch on the shore of what is left of the undergrowth of the mangrove roots, shacks, puddles of water, shit, and urine. Serpents who serve the Man with the Cloven Hoof. On a night full of lightning, thunder, and a profound celestial downpour, one of the dogs from the stone cave went into the shack in the mangrove swamp. He went in and spat in the face of one of the old women. In the morning, Abuela María was cleaning the rooms, and she went into Minerva's room and found her curled up with a woman with olive skin and the body of an African goddess. [Sum, sum, sum, sum sum Babaé.] In seconds Abuela María took the broomstick and fell on top of them as if she were killing cockroaches. The olive-bodied woman, between blows, managed to get dressed and run out of the house. Tía Minerva fled and hid on the roof until hunger overtook her, giving her no choice but to search for food in the kitchen, while still debating whether she liked women better than men. In this way it was discovered that my aunt Minerva also engaged in homosexual activity, THAT IS, that she was a lezzie, a dyke.

Felipe, indignant, decided to get involved.

"This is a matter between women. Let me talk to her," Pilar answered.

The next day Pilar put on a yellow suit and pastel shoes and purse, since she understood that problems should be resolved as elegantly as possible. The hardest part is picking out accessories, since yellow is a color that overpowers other colors. So the pastel shoes and bag and a string of Majorca pearls would give a somber touch to the outfit. She reached the grandparents' house and found Tía Minerva holed up in her room. It was a room with white furniture. The wardrobe, recently built by Abuelo, was a modern one, with wooden shelves and an infinite variety of stylish clothing and shoes. Tía Minerva was reading an article in *Vanidades* about how to make up your face to go out at night, and as soon as she saw Pilar, she cut right to the chase.

"I know why you came and there's nothing you can do. I feel like I'm half man and half woman and I don't care about the rumors. When I feel like a woman, I look for men and when I feel like a man, I look for women, and I will continue romping with whoever I feel like. By the way, that color of dress looks really good on you."

Tía Minerva straightened the hem of her pants, put on lipstick, and went out to the street. That was how Pilar learned to respect Tía Minerva and others of her ilk. She understood that there was nothing shady in her feelings; rather, they were simple, open, and fairly honest, for that matter.

"At least there's one happy woman in this family."

At home Felipe asked her, "Did you talk to Minerva?"

"Of course."

✳   ✳   ✳

"One of those dogs bit her."

"They say that when one of those dogs attacks you, you become unwomanly. The bad part is that the Rose of Jericho is no good for these things."

"Shhhh!!! Someone will hear you."

"We can't talk yet?"

"Shut up, the governor is talking . . ."

30

"To the good people of this island, prosperous in wisdom and tolerance, virtues that we want to grow stronger every day in our culture, I wish to dedicate this new era of the constitution to the great values of democracy, to strengthening everyone's rights, to stimulating the fight against poverty and unintentional ignorance. For some extremist groups, the most important thing has been that the others go away; for this government, that hunger go away, and to that end, the primary objective of my government is to increase production more effectively, the dilemma is investment and spending, when more is spent, less is invested, spending is the easy part, investing is the hard part, investing increases the temptation to spend, spending is not for the best, spending is the useless part of the dilemma, so it's about investing, just investing, only investing, investing to further the progress of everyone. The thought I want to convey to all of you, that is, the emphasis, the viewpoint, the thing I most wish to attend to, the action with the highest priority is this: government has a contractual obligation to the people who have placed their faith in it to struggle with the difficult problems of life, to establish the balance that feels appropriate between what the government should invest in expanding production directly or indirectly, and what it should spend, on providing services that do not in themselves expand production. Every day we will continue the established practice more harmoniously, as we are both the engine and the brake of misspending."

There were photographs, applause, autograph signings. There were extensive meetings in which the governor harped on about spending and misspending. A cocktail hour for the press was held at Palacio de Santa Catalina, more photos, more smiles, while in the town of Río Piedras a group of boys (serene, solitary, nonconformists) were reading Hugo Margenat, a young man who fancied himself a poet. Under the mahogany trees in the plaza, they clustered to hear his verses over and over. A jukebox in some bar was playing the latest from the hit parade. Those were the days when the Cuban consul in San Juan called upon the sanity and sense of all the Cubans who live in Puerto Rico and would soon be heading back to their country.

31

"As an official of the consular service of the Republic of Cuba, and therefore as the Colossus, the guardian, the defender of the interests of the citizens of Cuba, I sincerely hope that the change of government in our beloved Cuba will bring much-needed peace and tranquility to my people."

There was generalized jubilation and joy over the fall of Batista's government in Cuba. A special ship was sent to pick up the thousands of American tourists stranded by the general strike in Cuba that erupted because of President Batista's flight. Cubans in exile felt compelled to give thanks to the spirits and all the forces of the universe that aided such a happy enterprise, and they began to flock en masse to the grandparents' house.

"A prayer to ask for Fidel's well-being, comrade."

It was the request of the parishioners, usually ladies with hair dyed ash-blonde and thick layers of peacock-blue shadow on their eyelids. The exiles arrived in hordes, carrying their own chairs, and from early in the morning they took shifts at the entrance to the grandparents' house. Supporters of the movement that had triumphed in Cuba carried flags and posters, asking for RMC to intervene and cause President Batista's balls to explode. The grandparents' temple was crammed with Dominicans, Haitians, Venezuelans, and Spanish exiles carrying their instruments of gagá and voodoo, respectively. The neighbors began to complain about the ruckus going on in that house.

"It's like a Pentecostal temple. It's high time the police came in and shut that con man down."

The complaints to the nearest police headquarters, asking that order be imposed in that house, were ongoing; and on top of it all there was the rumor that the temple could very well be a Communist club in disguise. The Secret Service got involved, and Víctor was notified that he would be covering the case of the temple. Yes, that's right. Víctor himself, in the flesh. Víctor, alive and kicking. Víctor, who after many years had come back to the island with Tía Carmen and their children, now a specialist in underground battles.

"You're going to do surveillance on my own family? You have no shame!" his wife said.

"Don't be silly. The reason I accepted this mission is precisely that: to throw the government off track. I don't think there's anything going on at your house besides meetings where a few nutcases talk with the Great Beyond. Beginning with the biggest nuts of all, your mother and father. So please don't you come to me with your customary little sniping. Do you really think I'd be capable of building a case against your parents?"

"Dear, you are capable of anything," his wife said as she deposited a kiss on his cheek.

Víctor immediately gave instructions to police headquarters that they should watch the house closely, especially during apparitions of the spirit they called RMC: "What we do, the silence knows. But that's what we should all do together, those who have been convinced forever and those who are becoming convinced, those who are getting ready and those who are putting the last touches on their work, those of yesterday and those of today, those who work and those who do not. There is little time and great danger. They are tenacious and they watch us and divide us, so we shall watch them also, but prudence dictates that sanity is required."

"Compadre, you sound like a broken record. All that poetry of yours, no one understands it. These people, they come to hear news of their loved ones, to hear some clairvoyant message to tell them how many political prisoners, how many desaparecidos there are, how many children have died, how many military garrisons are on guard, how many backups, how many weapons, if there's food and clothing for everyone or if it's in short supply, what medicines are needed, how many whistle-blowers are lurking about—that is, what their chains are. The news of those who walk at night dragging their chains, carrying pain in their souls and hiding their sorrows," Eusapia Palladino answered.

"Tell me how my husband is doing in the slammer, sir, that's all I want to know."

"Be quiet."

"What's going on?"

"Shut up."

"I said what's going on, for Heaven's sakes?"

"Blast it, you're such a pest. Can't you see the fuzz is snooping around?"

"Wait just a moment, this is a democracy. That's why I left Cuba; they sold me this place as a paradise. And now it turns out you can't even speak. I want to know how my husband is."

"You've seen what people want to know!" Eusapia Palladino shouted at RMC.

32

Now elderly, the grandparents were less and less able to maintain order in the midst of the chaos of spirits, especially when dealing with requests having to do with the island of Cuba. The grandparents were still kind and consoling, but they didn't have the strength to manage the crowd and the demands of the living. To make matters worse, the souls of the temple were agitated because the disorder at the spiritist sessions was such that they could barely close the meetings with the prayers necessary to send the spirits to sleep the sleep of celestial dust. So it was very common to go visit the grandparents' house and suddenly feel the subtle presence of a spirit behind the kitchen trash can, or a tentative transparency on the other side of the shower curtain. Once I caught on, I would scare them away by shouting and waving my arms. The poor souls in agony could hardly cross the infinite when frightened, and mewed like newborn kittens. Even the crickets that scurried around in search of scraps of breakfast would flee every time they heard the ruckus.

In every corner, crack, hole, closet or wardrobe behind Minerva when she took a bath, next to some Spanish singer who was rehearsing "Qué bonitos ojos tienes" with Felipe in the yard or in the kitchen, you could find some spirit prescribing magical recipes. I listened to the spiritual beings' whispers, found a paper and pencil, and wrote down the recipes for

1. making a man love you,
2. making all men love you and triumphing over all your rivals,
3. making yourself extraordinarily loved,
4. making women desire you,
5. making all men and all women love you,
6. easy secrets for making people love you,
7. more secrets for the same thing,
8. another one to make a young single man love you,
9. making a widow fall madly in love with you,
10. seducing a married woman,
11. another for seducing a widow,
12. making a young single woman love you,
13. to stop a man from going around with other women,
14. to stop loving a man.

The souls seemed to be witches disguised by transparency, but they were really just beings affected by lack of direction. These souls turn into incongruent spirits, and incongruent spirits are hard to discipline. The spirits take over the neighborhood, frightening the elderly, children and animals; seize the money hidden in cookie tins; trap the smallest children to play with them like ping-pong balls; kiss animals on the mouth, leaving green running sores like headless toadstools; swing from the mango trees; and produce yellow shit that they crap on houses and the cupolas of churches.

"This temple has lost its composure; all seriousness is gone," RMC said.

"Compay, you need to realize what this is about—life and death, the rest is just trimmings. So shut your trap," Eusapia Palladino answered.

All the disorder was not intentional, but rather the direct consequence of the chaos in the temple. The rest of the family was upset because the peace and order in that house were being disturbed, and they demanded that Tía Minerva and Fernando stop pissing around and pay a little more attention to the bedlam in that house. Tía Carmen suggested that perhaps it was time to name a new president of the temple. "First off, don't even consider me because I'm very busy keeping an eye on my husband; it goes without saying that we can't count on Claudia Luz. Don't even think about Fernando and Minerva; those two are in another world. The only one left is Felipe; since he's the oldest, he's the best one for it."

Felipe! Felipe, who cared little for spiritual things. Felipe, who didn't understand a whit about transparencies. Felipe, a mí plin y a la madama dulce coco. Felipe que ni te vi ni supe dónde estabas. Felipe, who went to the spiritist sessions seldom, using his travels as an excuse. Felipe, who when he did attend the spiritist sessions, it was to hook up with one of the ladies.

Pilar could not get over her surprise. It meant that the spirits would come in and out of her house without permission, that they would be able to observe Pilar close up, they would be able to notice her careless offering.

That night my mother submerged herself in hot water and floated for a long while. Grief overcame her suddenly. She got out of the tub and picked up her vial of barbiturates, opened it, took out a pill, and went to sleep.

The next day I found her on the floor of the living room, going through a box decorated with shells and full of old photos and souvenirs. The rocking chair faced the window, the morning light slipped through the curtains, and the television was turned to the *Ed Sullivan Show*. Pilar grew old before my eyes, her forehead wrinkled, her crows' feet grew more pronounced, and her lips pressed together, trying to hold in a torrent of sorrows. I stroked her forehead and offered to help sort the little box. She kissed the palm of my hand, and two tears slid down her cheeks. The woman in front of me was my mother, and yet she wasn't; rather, I was her mother; Abuelo Cristóbal was her mother; the spirits, my father, and all of us were my mother's mother. Pilar passed the photos of my birth, photos of family parties, photos of her wedding. She found the newspaper chronicle of the death of Bella Juncos. She remembered her in her walks through the parks, through the streets and the plazas. She remembered their long conversations, their intense embraces, the poems with carrots and onions, Neruda's dark sea, and Juan Ramón's poems with his young Platero jumping through the mountains.

In the dark corners of my memory, I remembered the afternoon that Pilar went to visit Bella Juncos's tomb. That day she wore a fitted white linen suit with a matching belt. I climbed into the old Plymouth without being invited, and she didn't even notice. On the way, we went to pick up Tía Minerva. Tía Minerva wore capri pants, an off-the-shoulder blouse, and high-heeled shoes that matched the blouse. Pilar cleared the leaves and dried branches off the tombstone and Tía Minerva touched up her lipstick. The strong sun illuminated the afternoon, and the hot, dry grass was to the point of bursting into flame. You could just distinguish a row of houses from the cemetery, when the wind suddenly pulled the bushes into the center of the sidewalk. A wisp of cloud became a dark blanket, threatening to rain, but the wind lightened the way. Nothing could be heard in the cemetery besides the sound of Pilar's hands as she scrubbed the stone; besides my sneezes when the grass was stirred up; besides Tía Minerva's heels sinking into the dirt; besides a mangy dog sneezing near one of the Carrións' tombs; besides Pilar's hoarse voice as she said, "Fuck it! Bella, you had the sense to go when you felt like it, and the bravery to choose the death that most appealed to you. The only mistake is that you're dead."

The rocking chair stayed in front of the window, and a ray of shining sunlight slipped through a crack in the curtains until it touched the table in the middle of the room. The television stayed on, tuned to the *Ed Sullivan Show*. My dear viewers, at that moment Fidel Castro (thin, bearded, wearing an olive-drab uniform) made his entrance accompanied by the young Che Guevara. Behind them was an entourage of bearded men who seemed not to have bathed in days. Ed Sullivan, horrifying with his gigantic stiff neck, asked, "Well, Fidel, how was your visit to Harlem? And by the way, do you plan to buy some new clothes before you go back to Havana?" Ed bid farewell to the young men he described as "revolutionary youngsters."

Pilar picked up her purse, brushed the hair out of her eyes, hugged me, and left the house. Suspecting the worst, I called Tía Minerva. True, my mother did not return for three days. What did Pilar do for those three days? I don't know. I do know that my father walked around dazed, lonely, desperate, and with the strange feeling that he had lost a valuable treasure. Felipe went out to the streets and searched for Pilar all over the country. Day and night were not enough to fight time and the suspicion that something dreadful was happening to his wife. Terrified and like a wolf in the midst of a wild ocean, my father tried to break the barrier of silence that had overcome us all, lying across the island like a rug that needs cleaning.

"My child, Tía Minerva is here." I curled up on her lap, and for three days we moved in and out of the world of black dreams, crossing heaven and earth, hunting through animals' mouths and all the vegetation.

Felipe found Pilar; no one knows where or with whom, but they returned to the house together, holding each other, curled together, arms linked, like two peas in a pod. "You're the one I love, mi negra! The others are just unsweetened guava pastelillos. I want that to be clear. And besides which, I guarantee you that there will be no spiritist temple in this house. They'll have to find other lodgings," my father proclaimed.

Pilar hugged me and I hugged Felipe. The three of us stood there quietly, looking at the moon and its rays of light. Felipe, Pilar, and me.

33

A few months later, both grandparents slipped into a delirious waking dream. Abuela María played with her own shit, and Abuelo Juan had a lot of trouble finding his penis when he felt like urinating. They remembered their childhoods and confused the past with the present. The family decided to put them in separate bedrooms and immediately fixed up two rooms, one for each of them. An enormous amount of medical equipment and supplies arrived at the house, and Tía Claudia Luz devoted herself to taking care of the old folks with the precision of a space-age nurse.

One night, Abuela María, tired of all her ailments, simply said, "I am no longer myself; this is someone else inside my body." And she bid farewell to her physical body.

Abuelo, who always found out about everything, was immediately informed of his wife's death by the souls, and decided that without her he could not continue on the terrestrial plane. That night, he rose from his bed, leaned over to the dead woman's ear, and said to her, "I am not myself without you. I am someone else, someone incompetent and confused." He returned to his bed, closed his eyes, and stopped breathing.

Eusapia Palladino brought a chorus of nymphs, who invaded the house with their laughter. She took the grandparents' spirits and taught them what they needed to know to learn to fly. At the same time, RMC convoked the White Brotherhood of Tibet and the goddess Janus to discuss the future of the temple. The great-aunts, apprised of the situation, arrived from New York carrying seven suitcases of the season's latest fashions, a metal box of 45-rpm records, and a bag of the season's finest cannabis. The whole family went to the airport to meet them. When they reached the house, they sized up the situation at a glance and went into the kitchen. They fixed vegetables, codfish and avocado, and a raisin cake with a pinch of cannabis. Tía Minerva served a digestif. Claudia Luz, exhausted, lay down to take a siesta. Tía Carmen gave coffee to Víctor, while he looked flirtatiously at Pilar. Fernando went to the roof and began to sing, "Comprende que mi corazón ha sido burlado tantas veces, que se ha quedado mi pobre corazón con tan poquito amor," and Felipe went to pick up Abuelo Cristóbal. Pilar helped with the dishes, feeling Víctor's gaze on her back.

As always, the family had to make an expedition to the cemetery to find the colorless wall that acts as the boundary for the dead, and to scrub the family tombstone. The great-aunts volunteered to clean the tomb, and Pilar asked me to accompany them to the cemetery. I asked, "Can I invite Goyo?"

"Yes," Pilar answered.

The great-aunts insisted on taking my portable record player and the box full of records, and with great effort we all managed to get into Goyo's sports car. On the way, we ran into That One, who helped us with the package. Opening the iron gate—stiff with rust, walking up the main path, and reaching the guardhouse was always an adventure. On both sides.
the elaborate mausoleums
              of the well-to-do families

a little well full of mosquitoes
and water lilies,
fruit trees all over the area.

We reached our family's tomb and put the record player on
top of one of the neighboring tombs. The aunts caressed the tombstone several times. They opened the record player and installed
two batteries. The next moment, the best tango music ever heard
in that area poured out of it.

That One had stopped under a guava tree, "Just in case you need
me for something," and suddenly he began to sing "La Cumparsita."
Goyo disappeared, and a while later came back with some beers.
The chaos was such that This One, That One, and the Other
approached the stone and began helping to pour liquid on the
cold surface, scrubbing and splashing the family stone and the
nearest tombs and mausoleums. The amount of water was such
that it began to run down the sidewalks and paths of the cemetery, depositing itself in the canals of the mausoleums until it
reached the crucified Christs and Virgins of Macarena.

The day of the burial, all the parishioners of the temple wore
white. The ladies with their fans and parasols and the men with
their straw hats followed the hearse on foot. Goyo brought his
sports car, and I climbed in with him. That One with his drum
and someone with a conga joined the procession. So many people
showed up for the occasion that it looked more like a Palm Sunday procession. Several undercover police officers under Víctor's
command mixed with the funeral cortège. The conversations at
the meetings between those who had made hours' journeys by
bus, public car, or on foot, mixed with the banners of delega-
tions of exiles from Cuba, the Dominican Republic, and Haiti.
The members of the OZ Project put in an appearance, as did
the members of the lodges and the Patronage of Masons' Wives.
The undercover officers paid attention to all the conversations;
in addition, Víctor brought his camera. Minerva and I wore the
latest styles from El Imperio, one of the most elegant clothing

stores. Fernando, with the Los Hispanos trio, accompanied the service, performing all the boleros in his repertoire, ending with an a capella rendition of "Comprende que mi corazón ha sido burlado tantas veces, que se ha quedado mi pobre corazón con tan poquito amor."

My dear readers, the funeral convoy took Calle Santa Cecilia and turned left on Calle Eduardo Conde. It passed Facundo Bueso School, the School Supply Store, the house of Miss Valentín (my home ec teacher), and doña Matilde's bar, El Ausente. As a gesture of respect, doña Matilde turned off the jukebox. Víctor went into the bar and photographed the people going into and out of the latrine. He came out of the bar and photographed the parishioners, their parasols and umbrellas, the flowers, the fans, the legs and handbags. When he saw Abuelo Cristóbal carrying some paper cups, he photographed Abuelo's belly. He photographed Felipe and Minerva carrying a case of pitorro rum. He took a full-body photo of Tía Carmen, and when he saw Pilar, he took a portrait of her ass. The procession passed by Caimary School and the X-rated movie theater, where the billboard announced the latest picture starring Lourdes Vázquez, the pornographic film star, and Víctor took a full-body photograph of her.

San Juan, Beijing, New York, 2003.

THE DARK OF THE MOON

Memory produces a repetition of experiences that are often hallu-
cinated, like the dark side of the looking glass. I remember a wide
territory, like a dry, lonely plain, and a vast territory filled with
little yellow flowers huddled close to the earth. Life, perhaps, is a
consequence of the chaos of those flowers, unable to free themselves from the earth.

·